WESTERN ~~MIS~~ADVENTURES OF YIA YIA AND LUCEY

Patricia M. Linaris

outskirts
press

Outskirts Press, Inc.
http://www.outskirtspress.com

Paperback ISBN: 978-1-9772-0763-0
Hardback ISBN: 978-1-9772-0773-9

PRINTED IN THE UNITED STATES OF AMERICA

Dedication

To My Book Club Buddies: Alicia, Cathy, Debbie, Fran, Jo, Joan, Joanne, Linda, Pat M, Sharon and Val. What a group !!!

Table of Contents

#1

Yia Yia

The Box! That box!! That mysterious box!! It has me crazy always wondering what it contains.

A small jewelry box tied with a pretty red ribbon, I briefly held it in my hand before Sarge snatched it back. I was stunned, just about ready to open it when zip, it was gone.

We were standing in one of the exam rooms in the Veterinary Hospital. I just told Sarge that my curious meter was on overdrive regarding the box. Then he took it out of his pocket and handed it to me. I might add he had a big silly grin on his face when he did so.

The very next moment as I was ready to open it, he snatched it back. Claimed that this was the wrong setting and wanted to present it at a different, more personal setting.

Say what? I did agree that the timing might be off a little. We were at the hospital rescuing Lucey's poodle friend, Dottie.

It's a long story, suffice to say that the poor dog was dognapped by a delusional man, and then brought home to a hostile wife. The man believed that Dottie (the poodle) was his reincarnated first wife and decided that the three of them, his current wife Doris, him, the dognapper Rick and Dottie, who was actually Lulu, were going to be one big happy family.

I hope you are paying attention because it can get confusing. I'll try to give you the Reader's Digest version.

It seems that Doris was extremely jealous of the relationship between Rick and Dottie. Dottie wasn't too happy either. Fighting for her marriage, Doris decided they need some alone time away and booked a trip of the Queen Mary 2 for a second honeymoon, sans the dog.

Unfortunately, Rick couldn't bear to be apart from Dottie and managed to bring the dog on the trip without Doris's knowledge. Pointless to say it wasn't a happy moment when Doris found out. In fact she became suicidal; actually make that canine-a-cidal.

After a while and a few incidences the situation became clear to the powers in charge. It was discovered that Rick did indeed dognap Dottie and plans were made to reunite her with her family and the little girl so anxious for her return. Dog Dottie was in the Veterinary Hospital to get checked out while plans were made for her trip home.

Unfortunately, that was not good enough for Doris who still saw Dottie as the usurper of Rick's affection had decided to eliminate her, permanently! Disguising herself as an employee, she gained entrance to the veterinary hospital after it was closed for the night. Upon entering, she proceeded to assault the tech in charge, locking her in an exam room and went to finish off Dottie for once and for all.

Little did she know that Dottie, aka Lulu wasn't going to go easily? Nope, after trying to feed the dog-poisoned meat that Dottie refused, Doris desperately tried injecting her with something. Dottie managed to get out of her cage and began running wildly around the hospital with Doris in hot pursuit.

All the other animals started barking and making such a racquet that the cacophony finally got the attention of the employee in the back. He happened upon the scene and immediately called 911.

Doris was subdued, arrested and led off to be psychiatrically evaluated. Sarge then was notified and I went with him to make sure Dottie was all right. That's how I happened to be in the treatment room and thus how I almost found out what was in that mysterious box.

So now that you are up to speed with that whole scene, it still leaves me not knowing what is in that suspicious box. Of course I automatically think it's a ring. Why else could Sarge need a more 'personal' setting? I go between being flattered and being annoyed. What hubris!! He managed to get his farting problem somewhat under control but marriage? With him? Marriage? Not that I'm not a great catch, you have to agree I have liven up his life. Of course it would be nice to have someone to yell at from time to time. Lucey just doesn't cut it. She sulks and two minutes later guilts me into giving her a treat. Nope, she doesn't speak English either. Sarge does have the advantage there.

I think I will play nonchalant and ignore the whole box business for a while. I'll let him twist and turn in the wind. He'll be begging me to open that box.

Yeah, but what then? I know, an extremely long engagement. Yep. Thanks for this talk. I feel better already.

Actually, you know it not necessary a ring. Hmm!! But what else could it be?

#2
Lucey

I'm back in the car traveling to the Garden State. So far Yia Yia has been pretty quiet. Not so when Sarge isn't around and it's just her and me. Oh no, she gets herself in a tizzy wondering about that box. I was supposed to run on stage after her Hula performance and present it to her, but she messed up so bad that Sarge took the box off my neck.

It would have gone unnoticed until that Budinski stagehand told Yia Yia all about it and said he was wondering what was in the box. Did she get it? That set off all this manic behavior that I have to suffer through. She's sure it's a ring and vacillates about commitment. Really, at this age she should be grateful that's all she has to worry about.

Enough about her problems, let's talk about me. I'm still upset about poor Dottie. I am sure we are some kind of 3rd or 4th cousin. She's so adorable it explains my genetic makeup. She's going back to her real family in Cleveland while we are headed home. Sarge said we might have to still keep a low profile until we know if Yia Yia is still in danger from all the unsavory characters she managed to tick off. I hope that doesn't mean I can't go back to my old neighborhood and pick up my messages. It's always the innocent that suffer, meaning Moi of course.

From what I understand the first incident began when Yia Yia organized make shift parade around her complex. She rounded up some of the neighborhood Bros and some bag ladies that were pushing their carts through the streets. She convinced them to march in her make shift band and bring cheer to her cranky neighbors. It didn't work out as planned because some of the Bros wandered into someone's home and was arrested for B&E. That's breaking and entering; I learned that from Sarge. At the Complex's Club House Yia Yia told the bag ladies to help themselves to what they needed. That resulted to the Club House being stripped bare. They, the ladies were charged with unlawful entry and stealing

After a concerned resident called the police, a paddy wagon was dispatched and hauled the marchers off to jail but not before threats and obscene gestures were hurled at a confused Yia.

Moving on is the motorcycle gang that she abetted with bank robbery and then managing to get them arrested. Admitting, I had a small part in that too. Add to that is the Rent-a-Guy business that obtained early releases for the inmates in San Quentin. Seems her co-operation with the authorities uncovered plans and resulted in an exposure of corruption in the prison system, guards and inmates alike. Got me thinking there has to be an assortment of other unsavory people she entrapped while traipsing though life leaving chaos and pandemonium behind.

So you see, she's a danger to be with, ergo the witness protection program until the authorities can get it all untangled. Here I thought I would be having a quiet life getting pampered and luxuriating in being the focus of a lonely old lady. Axe murders lead a quieter life.

I'm not even sure what name she uses for me. At first it was Lacey. Cute, but doable. Then for some reason it got changed to

Lucey. Huh? I still don't know why. But it gets better. She sometimes referred to me a mega-hemorrhoid. I'm still trying to know what that means. I thinks it's German or Swedish or some endearment in a foreign tongue.

Lately she has been referring to me as Penance. She often says, "Look who's here, my Penance." Sounds classier than Lucey. Actually, she shakes her head and devoutly says, "My Penance." I think she is finally getting what a wonderful creature I am.

So you see, in addition to all the other quirks that make up my existence, I never know from time to time what is my name. It's probably another symptom of her advancing years. Well, as long as she doesn't try to stuff me in those pajamas again, I can deal.

I just hope my doggie friends are missing me and Roscoe hasn't found a new squeeze. I was up for leader of pack before I was whisked off on that perilous cruise. Actually the ship's accommodations for pets were fantastic. I might even apply for Ship's Mascot just in case Yia Yia has to do time for her assorted misdeeds. I think Neil; her lawyer bailed her out of some of them. I'm sure there are others.

I wouldn't mind going back on the boat (That's how they refer to the ship) if only the Captain lets me steer once in a while. Can't do any worse than him; last trip he took us though a horrific hurricane. How hard could it be?

Oh well, back to looking out the window and searching for cats. Last I heard Sarge say is we have another 6 hours of driving. You know maybe it's nap time. Yeah. I'll look for cats later.

#3

Yia

Just a few hours to go and we should be back in Jersey. I can't wait For my long overdue hugs from the Dirty Dozen, I miss them so much; first the kids and then the hugs.

I pestered Sarge to let me drive but got the same all answer as before. "This is an authorized vehicle under my name, I rented it as a member of the police force and the only occupant in this car authorized to drive it. Besides, I know all about how you drive you so called 'Rocket Ship' around. So, no way Jose!"

Yadda, yadda, yadda. Me thinks he's afraid of my superior driving skills. The man never goes over the speed limit, always uses his directional signal, checks the oil, water and tire pressure before every destination. He should have worked in a gas station. Boring!

My 'so-called Rocket Ship' has a 400 horse power injection twin turbo engine and can go from 0 to 60mph in 5 seconds. It comes with a manual or automatic transmission, anti lock disc brakes, every camera possible on a vehicle, run flat tires, lots of air bags, harness restraints and a ski bag. In addition, I have a moon roof that allows me to check for alien ships and rainbows, plus lots of bells and whistles but most importantly, me the driver.

My last SUV was Big Red, this one I affectionately call Black Beauty or the Yiamobile depending on my mood. I love to drive and feel stifled by my inability to get Sarge to give me the wheel. How rude!!!

Eventually the boredom of the road lulled me into a nap. Something roused me and when I regained my senses a green mist and the awful smell of farts surrounded me.

I checked behind me at Lucey, she was sleeping on her side making little chirping noises and her legs were in motion going nowhere. She must have been dreaming of chasing a rabbit or a cat or a pork chop. Obviously she was not bothered by the stink. Then again she likes to roll in deer poop so what does she know?

I zeroed in on Sarge, giving him my evil eye; I accused him of asphyxiating Lucey and me. Right away the denials. He actually said it was Lucey who was emitting the foul odors.

I couldn't believe my ears. I started praying aloud for penance before I resorted to do bodily harm to Sarge, of course.

Lucey: Penance, Penance was Yia just calling me?

Lucey awoke barking, oblivious to the toxic fumes in the vehicle.

She raced between the side windows, searching for danger. Sensing nothing there, her attention turned to Sarge and me. Sarge was still denying he was the guilty party. He insisted it was Lucey.

Lucey: What did I do now?

I grudgingly admitted it might be a possibility, but added only a low down despicable person would put the onus on the dog. As it was, Lucey was long overdue for a walk. When I calmed down, I told Sarge we needed to stop at the next rest area to walk the dog. All I got for my request was a HRRMPH!

We pulled into the recreation facility in the Ramapo Mountain area. Sarge, Lucey and I stretched our legs and breathed in the fresh mountain air, almost home. I asked Sarge where was our next stop? Replying he said that his Captain thought maybe a hotel would be a smart place until all the information regarding the location of the baddies was known.

For how long? I needed to see my family and they needed my wisdom and guidance and chicken soup. I could almost hear my own bed calling me. Traveling is nice but honestly I could use a Sarge break.

That's when Sarge said that this was just a stop over and I wasn't to reach out to anybody, less I put them in danger. He had to find out the status of all the baddies that supposedly wanted to do me harm. His Captain and he would decide future plans.

Say what? Where's my input? I was losing my temper. I started praying aloud for patience. "Lord, give me patience now? Where is my patience?"

Lucey: Patience, whatever happened to Penance? Boy, she's really losing it this time. Can someone tell me what's my name now? Patience!

We'll see about this turn of events; so close and yet so far. I have no idea but Lucey seems to be losing it. She's all over me and acting strange. Well, strange for Lucey, if that's possible. If I ever needed patience, now's the time. Guess I'll just have to pray longer and louder.

#4

Sarge

The rest of the trip went smoothly. After Lucey had her walk there were no more stinky farts; the nerve of that woman automatically blaming me. Now I know how the innocent feel when they are unjustly accused.

Finally, I reached my commander and he directed me instead of going to a hotel to go to a safe house already prepared for our return. He felt a hotel would be to public knowing Yia Yia's penchant for attention. Good idea, I also thought her family could pay a visit cutting down on her anxiety on how they were faring without her.

In the morning, I have a meeting with my Commander and the fellows from the F.B.I. who are monitoring the locations of the suspects.

Based on that will be the decision on whether or not to continue Yia in the witness protection program. The Bros and bag ladies that she convinced to march around her complex and got into trouble, well they already finished their sentences. In fact the Judge that presided on those cases dismissed most of them. Yia Yia was a terrible witness and not very co-operative. They don't pose an imminent threat. As for the San Quentin group, they are mostly eager to get retribution from Shirley. She was the one who gave the special cookies to the inmates and guards. The whole thing escalated into an investigation of the prison system with many heads rolling. So Yia dodged that bullet.

Speaking of Shirley, she married George, her Greek chef and moved to a vineyard out west. She is living under the radar and George knows to notify us of any changes or any new people interested in Shirl.

No, the biggest danger comes from the Biker Boys. They already tried once to bump Yia off with a motorcycle accident. She eluded that threat and went along her merry way. However, when Lucey was spying on her via the nanolaced cookies, Yia accidently ran into them at a used motorcycle yard.

A small reunion ensued, as all the members were exuberant to see her. They figured she never ratted them out to the authorities and welcomed her back into their group. However their joy came to a quick end when the police showed up and hauled them away. On their way to jail came the nasty threats and fist waving. Yia was confused until she learned it was Lucey who was transmitting their whereabouts and every word. No, they are the most dangerous threat to Yia's safety and wellbeing. Maybe even to her family too.

A few of the bikers are out on parole and from the word on the street there is a contract out on Yia's life. How one person can cause a commotion wherever she goes is beyond me. I've seen it with my own eyes and still scratching my head on how she does it; a natural talent I guess.

Pulling into the safe house, I realized how quiet the neighborhood was, nothing unusual except for the van. It was parked across the street from the house and was running. Obviously, somebody was inside. Walking over to check it out, I realized that the house was under surveillance.

I pounded on the door and an old friend opened it. Fred, it was my old partner Fred. A few questions later Fred now semi-retired, told me he pulled the watch duty and was going to keep an eye on the safe house. I was glad to see Fred, I know he would look out for our backs but the van was so obvious. A little discussion later, we both agreed to a subtile stakeout.

Fred was informed of all the danger and threats that had Yia in the Witness Protection Program. He wanted to know if she was as notorious as advertised. Fred was pretty disappointed when I told him on the outside she appears to be a naïve, sweet mannered, friendly old lady.

It's just that she is a magnet to all kinds of problems and situations. "I think her good nature and unsophisticated approach to life lends her to be taken advantage of sometimes," I was shaking my head when I told him. It brought back some pretty vivid memories.

Truth be told it was chaos and pandemonium that followed her everywhere.

I invited Fred over to meet Yia at the end of his shift. Meanwhile, I went back to the car and took Yia into our temporary housing. I just hope she can stay out of trouble here.

#5

Lucey

I opened my eyes when I heard the Sarge say, "Here we are, home at last." Jumping up, I ran to the window so anxious to get out and check out my hood, but wait, this wasn't home. I didn't recognize the place. Then Sarge told Yia to stay put there was something he had to check out.

Well, yeah!! He went to the wrong address, the big dummy. I had to admit I was much more comfortable with Sarge doing the driving. I even got in some snooze time but he must have made a wrong turn somewhere, I guess Yia will straighten him out. I need to get back to my 'hood'.

I watched as Sarge walked over to a parked van and got in, meanwhile I had to listen to Yia complaining about Sarge not letting her drive. Frankly, it was a blessing. Yia's driving around in her Black Beauty/ Yiamobile taking curves on two wheels gives me the shivers. There should be a law preventing seventy-year-old people from peeling out at every red light, then going at warp speed to be the head of the pack.

I'm sure you have heard this, Yia always bragging to people how well behaved I am in the car, "She never even tries to sit in the front, and I can go from here to California and never know there is a dog in the car."

There is no way Jose that I would go in the front to the suicide seat. I can barely keep from having a panic attack just getting in the car.

How the parents of the Dirty Dozen allow her to drive around their children, I have no idea. One day she almost had a head on collision with a huge fire truck, that's when she had her convertible and was out cruising with Christopher. I bet that shortened his life span a few years. Glad I wasn't there. I wouldn't ever get near that car let alone in it. A convertible, you know why she traded it in? Let's keep this amongst ourselves; I have to live with her. Anyway, she realized that she was falling into the car and had to pull herself out. Didn't think it looked cool. Can't imagine how many lives were saved by that decision.

There are times when she takes me out and we have to get gas. Once she stops at the pumps and the attendant comes over, I start immediately scratching and clawing at the windows looking for someone to rescue me. Occasionally she lowers the window just a bit and I try to scramble out. But never make it. It's no use, it's always the same, "She's so friendly, does it all the time," is Yia's explanation of my frantic behavior.

Whomever it is that gassed the car just nods, hands her the receipt and watches while she peels out into traffic. I am so doomed.

I'm panting and hyperventilating just telling you about it.

I sure hope Sarge gets this mix up corrected. I can't wait to get back to my hood and catch up with all my messages. I hope my friends give me a welcome home party or at least a few bones.

Here he comes now. After grabbing our bags, Sarge gets Yia and me and proceeds to enter the house. "We've arrived, this will be our place to stay until we straighten out the situation."

Err, what situation? I'm innocent; I want to go back to the 'hood' to retrieve all my messages. They must be piling up by now and I won't be able to tell who's who.

Little did Sarge care; I was last on the list after Yia started in on him. "How long will we be here? Can my family visit? Don't I get one phone call? This place looks like a shack!!!" And on and on.

I dove for the couch and stuck my head under the cushions. World War Three was about to break out. Then I heard it, another name change. Now Yia was yelling for strength.

"Where's my strength? I need strength now!" Strength? Now I'm called Strength. I wish she get one name and stick to it. I'm getting confused.

#6

Yia

The house was stuffy and stale so that I promptly went over to the window to let in some fresh air. Immediately Sarge yelled at me to get away from the window and what was I doing there in the first place?

"I was trying to get some new air in here and let out the old," I told him. What came next was scary. Sarge told me that the window were all bullet proof and wouldn't open, all for safety reasons and learn to live with it. "Are you kidding me? Bullet proof? Who am I? Al Capone, Osama in Laden? I thought this was a stop over not a fort! Take me home to my house. I'm sick of all this cloak and dagger stuff and while I'm at it, I'm sick of you too!"

"Calm down Yia Yia, this is for your protection and that of your family. This is just a stopover until we find out where all the players are and their intent. This safe house is not just for you, it for anyone in witness protection. Get over yourself!" Then Sarge stormed off mumbling to himself about getting old.

Here I thought my life would get back to normal. Making chicken soup, driving my Yiamobile, spoiling my Dirty Dozen. I've got things to do, people to see, I'm not cut out to be running on the lam.

While I was enjoying my rant the doorbell rang and as I went to open the door, I was quickly pushed aside by Sarge who informed me that I was never to open the door and to get out of sight.

Woe is me, I am now Sarge's prisoner, all because of the cookies that were fed to Lucey without my knowledge or consent. That's right! If she didn't give away the Biker Boys location I would still be home listening to my arteries hardening. Thinking about it I realized that I am the injured party and deprived of my golden years with my family's adoration. As soon as I put on my support hose I plan to stomp around and loudly protest my injustices.

Fuming, I took a peek at the door and saw Sarge welcomed a fairly nice looking man. This looks interesting. After a few words, Sarge called me and introduced me to Fred. Seems Fred has been busy watching the house and used to be Sarge's old partner.

Lucey went over and sniffed his leg and gave him the all clear. Okay, I'll pull myself together and be cordial. Who knows, maybe I can get Sarge to take a break and I can get to know Fred better. Hmm!

Sarge introduced us and excused himself to go into the kitchen. I bet he needed to fart and was being polite. No stinky air for a while, he must be bottled up.

Now let's see. Fred has salt and pepper wavy hair and a good amount of it. It might be Hair Club for men or something but I'm not ready to do a deeper inspection, yet. I asked him about his family and he told me he was a life long bachelor and not attached at this time. No wife or kids, I wondered what he did for aggravation. Not aloud of course, to myself. See I am behaving. I asked him about the Sarge, how long were they partners, where did they work, did Sarge always fart? Background info for the bored Yia.

No big revelations, they were partners almost 15 years and

worked out a precinct in Manhattan and he didn't answer the farting question. I heard the Sarge stomping around in the kitchen, listening to every word I bet.

Fred told me that he was working part time and was assigned to keep watch on this house occasionally. He told me to relax that he or his new partner would keep an eye on me for 24/7 and make sure I was safe. I didn't think it wise to tell him my plans to murder Sarge first chance I got, TMI at this point.

Sarge popped out of the kitchen just as Fred said it was nice meeting me and gave me his emergency number. Sarge ushered Fred to the door, said he was going to walk Lucey and be right back.

I peeked thru the blinds as they made their way towards the van. A lot of head bobbing going on combined with looks back at the house. My ears were aflame. I know it was all about me. I'll try to be nice to Sarge when he returns. Get me some gossip about his former partner Fred. Nice looking with hair and no farts. A possibility.

#7

Lucey

Sarge leashed me up and took me outside where I could get familiar with my new surrounding. Not too many scents here, mostly nasty ones from cats, a few piles of deer and rabbit poop. Doesn't seem like too much in the way of wild life.

Fred was asking Sarge about Yia. Huh? Like personal questions, How long he knew her, her marital status, was Sarge involved? Say what? This didn't sound like police work. It was over the hill dating game info. Not one question about me, how rude!

Yia doesn't need anyone in her life, she has the Dirty Dozen and most of all she has me. What more could a person want? I was worried about Sarge and that box, now this. Talk about fatal attraction. The man must be desperate.

Sarge told him that he has known Yia for years, always bailing her out of one jam or another. That she has sent a few people around the bend. The one policeman who went into the fire department not to have to deal with her. Then the Psychiatrist that treated her and wound up having a total break with reality. The last two perps that thought they were dogs and are still in treatment.

Fred stood rubbing his chin amazed. At first he thought Sarge was joking but when he realized he was serious he broke into a big wide grin. "What a woman. If you're not interested, maybe I could get to know her when this situation is resolved. Wouldn't want to horn in on you action, Sarge."

I could tell, Sarge was hesitant to answer; he just mumbled a few words and finally told Fred that he would talk to him after Yia was safe.

It was agreed and Fred went back to the van and Sarge took me for a walk around the block. Very quiet neighbor hood; sort of creepy actually. Not one person outside or kids toys lying around. Where was everyone? I felt like I entered the Twilight Zone.

I did my business and tugged to get back to the house. Bad enough Yia has a soft spot for Sarge, now this new interloper. I know I complain about my living conditions and dealing with a hyper septuagenarian but it's what I got used to. We don't need anyone else in this mix. I am going to have to find a way to keep Yia Yia focused on me and forget about these Lotharios.

#8
Yia

Sarge came bounding back; Lucey was tugging him for dear life. I quickly closed the blinds and sat in a nearby chair, pretending to read a magazine I found on the nearby table. Upon opening the door Sarge let go of the leash and Lucey jumped up and started to annoy me. "Cut it out Luce and get down. What has her so riled up Sarge?" He ignored me while he was fiddling with the locks so he could sit and catch his breath.

"I don't know Yia, one minute we are having a nice stroll around the neighborhood the next thing, she's racing to get back here. Are you all right? Were you screaming or singing?"

"No I wasn't screaming and I'll have you know I have a beautiful singing voice. However, I wasn't singing or screaming. I was just sitting here reading a few articles." I informed Sarge. "Hmm, try holding the magazine right side up, you can get more info that way" he shot back.

Sure enough when I looked the magazine was upside down. Score one for the Sarge. As I was gearing up to say something clever, the doorbell rang. Sarge looked out and told me that Fred was off duty and was stopping by and try to behave myself.

"Really! How Rude! When am I not a perfect lady?" Sarge paid me no mind as he went to undo the locks and welcomed

Fred. Fred gave me a big smile and a wink as Sarge ushered him to a nearby chair.

"So Yia, I like to get a little background on the person or people I watch. You don't look like the typical witness protection subject. Sarge tells me there are a few perps that want to harm you. How come?" So Fred was curious.

I thought I should turn the table so to speak and ask a few questions of my own. Seemed fair to me. " Sure Fred, but first I have a few things I want to know about you. Let's share." I could tell this was annoying Sarge no end so I pressed on.

"No Prob," said Fred, "where would you like to start?" again with that wink. I was curious why he was still a bachelor and asked him that for starters. His answers were what I expected. Never met the right woman, got set in his ways, in his younger days had a roving eye and so on and so forth. Now he said he would love to settle down and enjoy a person to share his retirement years. Again that wink. The old goat was definitely flirting with me. I decided to use that to my advantage just to annoy Sarge. Hey what else was there to do around here?

Then he asked me how I landed in the witness protection program? Was I a criminal a snitch or whistle blower or something else?

Sarge interrupted at this point and explained that I uncovered the Biker Boys who robbed banks and now some are out and seeking retribution. "Not so, not so!! I never narced on them, in fact it was Lucey with all the fancy cookies you fed her that blew the whistle on them I was an innocent bystander and if you must know it's Lucey who is responsible for me having to miss the best years of my life with the Dirty Dozen. If I didn't go streaking in my body suit and get knocked out, I was going to be the poster sex idol for the over the hill crowd. Don't think I'm happy about missing my 20 minutes of fame. My adoring public has a short memory and my looks are fading with each day!" I lost it but Sarge had some nerve when he knew in fact that he and his cronies had Lucey spying on my every move.

I looked at Fred who at that moment was winking with both eyes; in fact it might have been blinking. He shook his head and for a moment I thought I saw his hair move. Aha! He had on a toupee. I had some suspicions that might be the case.

An awkward silence invaded the room and then Fred abruptly stood up and said he had to be going. Good, I was tired of all his winking and blinking; besides I had to get a few things straightened out with my protector, Sarge!

As Fred high tailed it to the door, Sarge walked past me to let him leave, mumbling under his breath about senility. I sure hope he was speaking about himself. There needs to be some air cleaning around here, the sooner the better.

A walk with Fred to his car calmed Sarge down a bit. When he returned he was not as feisty and there was no more mumbling. He went directly into the kitchen and started looking for dinner makings.

"I think you're mad at me Yia and think it was me that denied you your date with destiny. I'm sorry you feel that way, I was only trying to protect you from the baddies you stirred up and while I'm on it, there was quite a few. You have a natural talent for ticking some people off, me included."

Whoa! Glad he got that off his chest like he's Mr. Cool. I decided just to keep quiet and let him stew. You know the saying, 'Don't get mad, get even.' While his blood pressure was climbing down I was planning on my revenge. Looking back I think he's still mad at me for giving away his Oatmeal Raisin cookies, his fart regulators.

Doesn't matter that he had the whole ship affected by them, no it was my fault for giving them away. Well, it's just a guess but he's in a snit about something. The silent treatment will be my weapon of choice for a while.

He can talk to his buddy Fred or Lucey. I'm clamming up for a while.

#9

Lucey

Er…I don't know why I was in such a hurry to get back to this house; the tension here thicker than a pork chop. Yia doesn't do well cooped up, she's more of a free spirit and Sarge is constantly reminding her of her danger to herself and others. Others include me, I think.

I wish we could just go back home and I can pick up my messages and be Queen of the neighborhood again. This vagabond life is not my cup of kibble.

There's a small rumbling of blame shaming and Yia openly flirting with Fred that has Sarge's shorts in a bunch. I know she did it to annoy him but sometimes I feel sorry for him. Other than his farting condition he's not a bad sort. Actually the farts never bothered me. It's better than rolling in rabbit poo and having to have a bath in the sink. Farts just fade away.

I, myself was wondering what was in that box, I would have found out if Yia didn't career off the drummer and show the audience her rear end. Remember she had on the body suit tattooed with "Kiss My Butt" in the appropriate place. She got a standing ovation for that because the audience thought it was part of the act.

I was supposed to run on stage and present the box to her, but Sarge took it off my collar and now I stay awake wondering. Not really, but from time to time while I stop daydreaming of Bruno (he's my latest doggie heart throb) it sneaks into my thoughts.

At the rate of these two sniping at each other the revelation will become the eighth wonder of the world.

You know Yia holds me responsible for having to be in this Witness Protection Program. She had no idea I was transmitting her whereabouts until the squad cars all pulled up. I sure hope she realizes I used as an instrument of protection for her and Shirl. In fact I am still suffering from the eyestrain. Do dogs wear glasses? Maybe contacts, Yia wears them you know. Sometimes she mixes up the lenses and bounces off the walls until she figures it out. Thought she was stroking out until she switches them. One of the many crosses I bear.

Wit a sec... I hear some mumbling in the kitchen; I better go check it out. Last I knew Sarge was in there rattling around some pots and pans.

#10

Sarge

I have no clue where anything is in the kitchen. I opened the fridge and saw some steaks and chops and salad makings. I guess I'll start with that. I'm not a cook either so I wish Yia Yia would lighten up and come in here to bail me out. Opening cans is my best talent, that and ordering out.

Tomorrow we have a meeting with my Captain and reassessing this situation to decide on the next plan. Yia isn't making this any easier for me. Maybe it's time to hand her over to a new detective and take my retirement. Then I think of what to do and change my mind again. "What do you think? Lucey. I'm speaking to you."

Lucey sat there twisting her head back and forth, what did I expect? How could I decide my future based on what Lucey thinks?

Lucey, Welcome to my world. I twist my head from side to side and try to look intelligent. Actually I came in because I thought he was cooking and something would fall on the floor. I've been trying for years to get an angle on Yia but what I thought was a sweet old lady turned out to be an over the hill hyperkinetic lunatic. So again, welcome to my world!

Finally, I gave up and called for Yia to come and help. She has to eat too, you know. In she struts to the kitchen, opens a few drawers, cabinets then the frig. Takes out some bread, gets a jar of peanut butter, slams the top on the counter to open it, slathers some peanut butter on the bread, then gets a glass pours herself a glass of milk and sits down and eats.

All the while I stand there like a dummy and watch. Here I thought she'd whip up a home cooked meal. Speaking not word, she finished, stuck the dishes in the dishwasher and strutted back out of the room. I think she's mad at me for something and I'm still hungry. Well, I guess I can make a peanut butter sandwich and look for some dessert to round it out. I guess I deserve some of this, I could have leveled with her about the cookies but it wasn't my call to make. Actually her eating some cookies and overdosing her captors with them probably saved her life. She has no good reason to put it all on me. Two can pay this game; I refuse to be treated in this fashion. I have my pride too.

No more Mr. Nice Guy, I'm not speaking to her either. So there!

#11

Lucey

What about me? Where's my supper? Those two are so busy fussing with each other that they are totally neglecting moi!

Yia was sitting in one chair busy reading an upside down magazine and Sarge was at the opposite side of the room brooding.

I tried jumping on Yia's lap and got pushed off mid air, and then I tried the Sarge. He just gave me a stare and then it clicked. "Oh Lucey, I bet you're looking for your dinner? Let's go see what we have for you, maybe Yia would help too."

Lucey: Maybe if I play my cards right there may be a big fat pork chop in my future.

Just my luck as I was following Sarge into the kitchen, Yia abruptly got up and told him she would take care her dog and that she didn't need him buttering up her via the dog. Next she stormed into the kitchen and pulled out a bag of yucky dry food and proceeded to fill a bowl and with great effort and plenty of noise, called me to eat some.

She started once more with my new name; "I have no idea where I got my Patience from, must be a gift."

Duh, you got me and my sisters at Country Junction in Pennsylvania, then you called me Lacey, moved on to Lucey and know I don't know what my name is, Lucey, Patience, Penance,

Strength? I wish she'd pick one and stick to it.

After wolfing down the dry kibble, I went back to check out Yia.

Sarge followed right behind me and sat down next to her. He's a brave man!

He explained that she was right to be upset about the spy cookies but she did use them for her advantage too. Why couldn't they put it behind them and go see the Captain. By now her situation may have changed and maybe even call the family from the station. Perhaps they could make a plan for a get together.

I could tell that Yia was softening and admitted she was uptight about her future and missing the Dirty Dozen terribly.

What do you know? There is peace upon the land!! For a while at least.

#12

Yia

After a restless night of tossing and turning in the lumpy bed, I got up at sunrise and went to make some coffee. I am so anxious to go and get the report on the suspects that mean me harm. I can't imagine what I've done to get somebody so mad at me. I left Lucey snoozing away and was surprised to fine Sarge up and ready to face the day.

He was sitting at the desk reading and was drinking a mug of something. I sure hope it was coffee. I am having a Starbucks withdrawal and need my caffeine. I must have startled him because he got up abruptly and I think he went to reach for something.

I'm trying hard not to imagine what it could have been. He collected himself and told me he was surprised I was up so early. "Nothing like a good jump on the day. I can't wait to get this situation settled with your Captain and resuming my old life. Is that coffee by any chance and is there more?"

"Sure Yia I just made a pot and glad you're in better spirits this morning."

"Don't push your luck, it's the coffee I need now, we'll discuss my spirits when I get a cuppa,"I was starting to remember how annoyed I was with him.

Sarge told me we have an appointment at one PM with his

Captain and we'll discuss what is known about the supposed perps mad at me. Then we will plan what is to be done to protect me.

Actually, I just want to resume my old life and go home. I'll promise never to streak again. Getting in and out of that body suit was an ordeal and I'll break a hip if I try it again.

Sounds boring but its time to take a breather and get back to the Dirty Dozen. Goodness knows how messed up they must be with all that helicopter parenting they live under. I have to give them my best advice on living life to the fullest and enjoying themselves; within reason and lawfully, of course.

The day dragged on and I couldn't wait for One o'clock hour to arrive.

My future depends on the information I get today and my decisions. At last the little hand and the big hand on the old clock came together at noon; finally Sarge announced it was time to go.

Yea!!!! I took extra care to look as presentable as possible and even applied a second coat of mascara that sort of stuck together whenever I blinked. It gave me a real flirty look or maybe the beginnings of a stroke, one of those.

Fred pulled the van around and the Sarge and I got in and buckled up to go of course, downtown. Arriving at the precinct we pulled into an underground garage and Sarge quickly walked me to the elevator with Fred covering our rear. Talk about cloak and dagger stuff. Really!

We exited on the fifth floor and were greeted by the Captain and a couple of his deputies. Introductions all around then the Captain proceeded to take us to a conference room.

Overwhelming is the first word that came to mind to describe what happened next. There in that room was my family. The whole beautiful bunch of them, my children and their spouses and best of all my Dirty Dozen waiting for me. For once in my life I was speechless. I couldn't hug them fast enough and was amazed how they manage to grow so tall and beautiful with out my guidance. If I wasn't such a strong specimen of a human I think I might have fainted. My knees were trembling as it were and I had plenty of questions to ask. I stood staring in wonder and felt forever since I held them, I know it wasn't but my achy breaky heart couldn't get enough Yia Yia hugs.

As I was basking in all the attention and trying to answer all the many questions, I managed to look around. There was Sarge sitting with his Captain, Fred and the other deputies. All at once I realized that it had to be Sarge who managed this surprise for me. I gave him my broadest smile and he grinned that goofy smile back, then I got back at work spoiling the twelve young faces before me

Things finally calmed down and my one daughter suggested I tell the group all about my adventures on the ship. I bragged about coming in second place in the dance contest and gave a shout out to my partner Sarge. I toned down the talent show just saying it went over well. No sense in telling them about my disastrous ending. I didn't mention all the problems with Rick and his disturbed wife. For that matter I left out the part about being kidnapped and the special cookies that saved my life. ;that I'll relate when they are older and can take the shock.

The hours passed too quickly and soon one family after another came up for a big hug send off. I promised I would be careful and all that other good stuff.

It was time to hear what was the verdict on the people that wished me harm. According to the Captain the biggest threat came from the paroled Biker Boys. He felt the prison gang targeted Shirley and the neighborhood group had moved on to either bigger or badder or gone conservative with kids of their own.

Reality hit me square in the face and after seeing the family I knew I had to stick out this separation until it's resolution. I could never put the family in danger and so saddened I agreed to stay with the Protection Program and needed to know the next step.

To my surprise plans were in the works for me to go and visit with Shirley and her husband for a while. She now lives in a remote area on a vineyard in Oregon. Sarge agreed to accompany me and be my bodyguard. And to think I didn't even make him a peanut butter sandwich. I had a slight case of the guilts knowing how he must have planned this reunion for me.

The Captain suggested we travel by rail. I can bring Lucey with me and in 4 or 5 days we would arrive in Oregon, I was to have a sleeper while Sarge had the sleeper next to mine. We could have our meals in our room until Sarge checked out all on board and then we could go to the dining room. The Train stops at different stations where Lucey could be walked. It sounded like a great adventure and I would have plenty of reading time, just thinking about seeing the whole country was like a dream come true. Now that's a program I could agree to and arrangement were made as we spoke.

Truth be told I have been missing Shirley, we sure had some good times together. She was a really good sport about some of the mishaps. Good old Shirl, I know Lucey will be over the moon when she sees her; they speak the same language. Enjoy the same dog biscuits too.

Well, today has turned out to be quite a day, got to see all my family and now a cross-country trip. Maybe I should get some lottery tickets. It sure feels like my lucky day.

We finished up with the Captain got our itinerary and instructions on how I was to conduct myself. In other words I was to be low key and not bring attention to myself. Can I help it if I'm a people magnet? You would think that I control these God given gifts of allure. I'm not saying I don't use them to have a little fun but my Mom told me never to hide my light under a basket; something like that.

Sarge was quiet on the return to the safe house; I was feeling a little guilty for giving him a hard time especially after he arranged to have my family have a get together at the station house. Well, I'll concede one point for him; I might even try to be pleasant.

All our arrangements are being worked out and as far as I know, Shirley and her husband George have agreed to harbor us for the duration of time it takes to get more information of the baddies still mad at me.

I thought if I could explain the situation to them they would go away, but I got shot down on that idea. So Oregon here I come. What do people do in vineyards? I guess I'll find out. It sure will beat sitting around waiting for the next fart attack from Serge and/or Lucey. Life has to have more meaning than that.

Maybe I'll learn to pick grapes or make wine. You know I always have a glass or 2 at the 5 o'clock hour. Good for the heart. Good for my spirit too.

According to Sarge the trip should take about 4 days. We take the Lake Shore Limited to Chicago and then transfer to the Empire Builder for the rest of the journey. We both have sleeper cars next to each other and I will have Lucey with me. Meanwhile I'm stocking up on some reading material and writing Shirley a note. I'm so excited to see her. It seems like ages. Other than the pain of missing my immediate family, I know this is the right thing to keep them all safe. Maybe I should get a total make over and some plastic work done and come back incognito.

I'd still be the same Yia underneath all that stuff, so why bother?

This is my cross to bear for being so darn friendly and charming. I can see some of the Grands have the same traits. I'll have to warn them about the power of being too adorable. Well, almost back to the house, time to pack up again. Fred will be taking us to the train in the AM.

Oh wait a minute; Sarge just informed me that Lucey needs a vet visit. Something about getting rabies shot and whatever else she needs. I guess the Sarge will bring her, I'm not allowed outside by myself. Really!

So tomorrow I'll pack up our small possessions while Sarge has the pleasure of the Vet visit. Of all the things in life that are so important I can't imagine this being on the A list. I'm pretty sure Lucey is all up to date with her inoculations? This better not be one of those phony reasons to get her those spy cookies again. I'm wise to these shenanigans.

Thinking about it, I realize that maybe the plan is use Lucey as a monitor again. I'll figure it out once she starts with that staring stuff again. I'll figure it out.

#13

Lucey

Oh boy! Something is amiss. Sarge took me out for my morning walk and instead of leaving my deposit in the trash, he brought it back into the house. You know what I think? I think he plans to take me to that quack Vet. Yeah, he's up to something. He's been whispering to Yia while looking in my direction. This can't be good. I looked around for a fort but the best I could do was crawl under the bed. The good life with extra treats have put a little bit of extra plumpness to my lithe frame so it was no easy task getting under there. I'll just hang out for a while and maybe the moment will pass. No way Jose am I going. Last time that snooty nurse stuck me with two; I said two blunt needles in my tusch.

I had my listening ears on over time trying to catch a snippet of conversation but all I heard was the TV on in the living room. No way can those two keep quiet. My suspicions are right; they are hatching a plan right now.

I listened and listened and then I thought that maybe they forgot about me. That's not possible, I'm the glue that hold their lives together. The star of the show, where's the attention I need ravished upon me? Don't they care I'm missing? Why aren't they looking? Maybe I got dognapped. Hey, it could happen being as adorable as I am. Maybe they are canoodling? Nah, but then again Yia is still thinking about that box.

She's probably using her ancient feminine charms on him. He probably needs rescuing. I better go save him. Geez, it's tight in here.

I manage to struggle my way out and ran into the kitchen to find them and guess what? They tricked me! That's right! Sarge grabbed me and hooked my leash on my harness and dragged me to the car. Drats! How could I be so naïve?

We went out the front door and I marveled at beautiful gold carpet down all around the neighborhood but as I got closer I realized it was all the leaves that fell off the birch trees. Seems like fall is beginning and the days are getting shorter. Good, more time for me to sleep. I was trying my best not to think of where we were headed. Vets, yuck.

At least I wasn't in that smelly police car. This one had a nice cushy back seat and I didn't slide all around. In fact the Sarge wasn't his old farty self. Maybe he went to his Vet too.

Unfortunately the ride was short and I got dragged out of the car and into the office. The same snooty nurse was there and I tried hard not to make eye contact. Actually I thought when she turned around to walk us into the exam room I could nip at her fat ankle. Yeah, that's the best idea I had all day.

No luck, for someone so chunky, she was a pretty fast walker and Sarge kept me on a short leash. I'll wait until she comes back with her dull needles to get my revenge. Timing is everything.

Sarge explained to the nice lady Vet that I was there to go over my inoculations and get up to date with my rabies vaccine. I wondered what about him, I bet he needed a rabies shot too, Yia too come to think of it. Why is it always about me?

The lady Vet was all happy to see me and declared me perfect. Of course I knew that all along but I guess the humans I live with need to have reassurance. They are so insecure. Luckily, no shots, nope I was all up to date. It was kind of sad because I had plans for that nurse. Next time. I have a mind like a steel trap, I won't forget.

Well, back to the car and the drive home, almost. Oh No! Sarge is making a detour to that gray depressing building that has my old friends and the nerdy computer guy. They better not be hatching another plot for me to spy on Yia Yia. Last time I needed glasses from the eyestrain and Sarge was almost thrown over board. This guy (Sarge) is really looking for trouble.

As it turns out, the Sarge was there for a new supply of nano-laced cookies. I received a big pat on the head from Dudley who had to remark about my weight gain. That's one off my Christmas list. After the catching up, handshakes, good luck wishes followed us out the door.

I'm still concerned what Sarge has planned for the cookies, no more recruiting me for his projects. I live a shorter life span and need everyday.

I am anxious to see my bestest friend Shirley. I'm glad she's over her chicken obsession. We had a lot of fun together and she isn't always giving me orders like you know who. "Stop barking Lucey, you're giving me a headache. Stop rubbing your butt on the floor, it's not funny. Must you jump all over everyone we meet, it's embarrassing. Get off the table, it's not for dogs!" See what a restricted life I lead? Shirley's more of a free spirit. Good old Shirl. I can't wait to share some milk bones with her. I'm just wondering what a vineyard is. I sure hope they don't have any animals running around. I'm more of a city dog myself and in the country those animals do their business wherever and no one cleans it up. How unsanitary.

My first train ride, I think maybe I can hang with Sarge. Too much togetherness with Yia can wear me out. I'll keep you posted on the trip. Later.

#14

Yia

Sarge just left with Lucey to get checked out for our journey. I sure wish we didn't have to go. As much as I want to see Shirley I will miss all my family. Oh why did I ever streak? It seemed to be so much fun at the time. Well, you can't go back and redo, so I'll just have to soldier on.

That pesky doorbell rang, I peeked out and lo and behold it was Fred standing there.

"Hi Fred, what's up?"

"Nothing too much Yia, just thought I could have a few words with you before Sarge gets back."

This sounded strange to me but interesting.

"Ok let's sit, did you want some coffee or something?"

"Oh no thanks Yia. I'm fine. Just had an idea I thought I will run past you. OK"

"Sure Fred, idea away."

"I am volunteering myself to go on your trip to see your friends and not wait out the threat here at home. I know you and Sarge don't always see eye to eye and I think we, you and me have sort of struck a more amenable comfort zone."

"So Fred, you want me to dismiss Sarge and you and I travel

together? Is that your idea? You know Fred that Sarge and I have a long history and if you hurry and leave I won't tell him of our discussion."

"Hold on a sec Yia, maybe I got some mixed signals. I'm trying to do you a favor here."

"No Fred, you're trying to weasel a vay-kay at the public expense and use your charm on me. No way Jose! And further more the Sarge and I are practically engaged! I just haven't given him my answer yet. There are lots of things for me to consider. So why don't you and I part amicably and forget this conversation happened unless you want to be in a body cast for Christmas."

"Geez, Yia don't give me threats, I'm just trying to get to know you better that's all and I see how you and Sarge act. Not too much love going around there. You're missing out on a great time, I'm a fun guy and could show you a good time."

"Sounds like an opportunity. Now I'm going to show you something too."

With that I got up and showed him the door. He had the nerve to turn and wink at me on the way out. He sure has a big opinion of himself. Wow what a weasel!! I have half a mind to tell Sarge about this but I better keep it to myself. No sense in causing more angst in this situation. We'll be gone tomorrow and that will be that.

Too bad Lucey's not here, she could nip him in his ankle or something. Sarge is not my dream man but he does take care of me. He's gotten me out of plenty of scrapes and I'm or saying anything one way or the other but that box still has me curious and I'm not quitting until I find out what's in it. You know what? Now is a perfect time for me to snoop. He must have it somewhere. Maybe I should tidy up his room.

Oh no, they're home already. What bad luck! Lucey looks happy, guess she didn't get any shots. I'm going to calm down and wait for another opportunity to look for that box.

#15

Fred

As soon as I got back to my van I started to phone my contact with the head of the Motorcycle gang. I hated to admit that Yia Yia didn't fall for my charm and good looks. She's probably a little blind at her age.

I was offered a lot of money to get between her and her watchdog, Sarge. I was going to retire in style and now I have to tell Rocco that I failed this mission. Maybe before I do that I can get Sarge to take a break or come down with a virus or something. I would hate to pass up a big bonus just to watch a little old lady take a train ride. Rocco swore he wasn't going to hurt her just maybe show his gang that he can deliver on his promises. A little scare and then let her go. No harm, no foul.

Just then I spotted Sarge's car pull up and I'll go and talk to him before he gets into the house.

"Hey Sarge, wait up, I need to ask you something."

"Everything all right? Any problems?"

"No, no Sarge, no problems at all, in fact I just checked on Yia and she's fine. I was just wondering if you want to take a break and I could be her bodyguard for the trip. You've been on this detail for a while and she seems like a handful."

"Fred, you can't imagine the energy this woman has, you're

right, she's a handful. But thanks for the offer, I might regret not taking it but as of now, I'm good. Thanks again, Buddy."

"If you change your mind, the offer stands, Ok?"

"Ok."

"You know Sarge, there was some talk about you wanting to get relieved from watching Yia. I went over before and volunteered to take your place but she wasn't into it. What's going on between you two? Anything good? She said you were practically engaged."

"Hmm, surprised she thought that Fred. No, I'll take her out to see her friend Shirley. I want to see how's she's doing then I'll decide my next course of action."

Rats, before I call Rocco, I think on this some more. Sarge and I go way back. I was teamed up with him when we both rookies and started out on the force. We were a good team, worked well together. I was with him when his wife became ill and passed away. It was a difficult time and being childless, he was pretty much alone. He started eating a lot of junk food and got this farting problem. It got so bad that he was called Farticus. Not to his face of course, but it was the headquarters nickname for him.

I think I will approach this from a different angle; the old lemon to lemonade theory. I'm just glad I had the chance before Yia told him I was trying to take his place. Sort of gave my little performance a different slant. Now I'm going to think of another way to get her away from him for a little chat with Rocco.

#16

Yia

I watched as Sarge pulled up with Lucey. He was headed towards the house when Fred called him over. I wonder what kind of story he was going to tell, I'm sure it will be altered.

Sarge stared over at the house. There was some head bobbing and nodding that I couldn't interpret. I bet that Fred gave him a watered down version on how he planned to backstab him.

I wasn't going to tell Serge that his so-called friend was trying to cut in on the trip, without Sarge of course. I'm not even used to being watched day and night by Sarge, forget that self absorbed, self centered Romeo that wanted to take his place. Oh why am I such a magnet to men?

I just want to go home and start my career as the sex idol for the senior crowd. Maybe even a new magazine. I can be a writer and publisher. I'll run it by Shirley when I see her. I bet she'll have lots of topics for the start up publication. Background life stories about love among the 60 plus crowd. Such possibilities.

I packed my luggage; I didn't even get to open all of it. I was going to snoop around Sarge's stuff but interrupted by Fred trying to horn in on the trip west. I'll tell Sarge at a later date but as of now I am getting anxious to see Shirley and have some girl talk. No sense stirring up the pot.

Sarge came in after a while and told me everything was in place for our trip. Fred was going to take us to the train station in the morning and our tickets would be ready for pick-up there. He mumbled something I didn't quite catch and when I asked him to repeat it, he said it wasn't important and went to his room.

Of course, I couldn't let it go, I followed him and asked if there was something he wanted to talk about, he seemed troubled. Maybe I had it wrong, maybe Sarge didn't want to go and had Fred sweet-talk me into taking his place. That way it didn't appear that Sarge was bailing on me. Men, just when you think you have them figured out they confuse you more.

He sat fidgeting on the edge of his bed, looking down and nervous. I never saw this side of him before, he's always calm and in charge.

"I think I sent out some mixed signals Yia and now I have to straighten them out. I think I told you that when we were leaving Canada off that fateful cruise that I thought you might be better off with someone else being your body guard."

My heart sunk and I could feel my eyes welling up. I was right, he put Fred up to taking his place and I was as rude as I could be to him.

Then Sarge went on, "You know, Yia that you and I go back a long way and I have come to know most of your quirks and I even got used to Lucey."

Lucey "What about me? I've taken many of your farting attack blames. Some pal you are."

I could feel myself getting more and more lost, I hadn't realized how much the Sarge was in my life. How I came to depend on him rescuing me in some of the jams I got into. Now he's leaving me and I will miss him dearly. I held back a sniffle as I watched Sarge's head bowed and staring at the floor.

"What do you say Yia? If you want to change bodyguards at least let me take you to see Shirley. I want to see how's she's doing and make sure you will be in good hands once I turn you over to someone else."

That's it? That's his problem? Oh for goodness sake. As he looked up he could see I was smiling. I was afraid of him not being in my life. He was a fixture and he even like Lucey.

Lucey, I'm really confused.

"Sarge, I want you to be my body guard and protector as long as you want. I barely have you half broken in and now you want me to start over? No Siree, this job is yours and there's no quitting now. Just get over yourself and put on your big boy shorts and stop moping. You're getting me worried." With that I stomped out of the room hoping I gave him time to save face and collect himself. I couldn't tell him how lost I would be without him.

Lucey, Could somebody explain to me what just happened?

I felt like a big weight was lifted off my shoulders and hoped

Sarge would be his old self again; of course without the farts. Lucey trailed behind me, I think she's looking for treats. Maybe I'll cook tonight just so I don't get rusty.

I had a restless night, sleeping in fits and starts. I was too anxious to see Shirley, sorry to leave my family and worried about Sarge's mood. As I tossed and turned I saw though one eye the faint light of dawn peeking through the window blind's slats. Ignoring the inevitable, I punched the pillow, tightly close my eyes, rolled over to my other side and tried to get in a few more winks.

No Luck! I might have made it except my nose picked up the unmistakable scent of freshly brewed coffee. I paid no attention to it but then my stomach started to growl and my caffeine addiction forced me out of bed.

Lucey was still snoozing away. She probably thought I was doing a bathroom run and would be right back. I wish!

I stumbled into the bathroom, brushed my teeth and tried to smooth down my bedhead. I had no luck in that department. My hair stood straight up in some places and looked like I spent the night in a wind tunnel. Grabbing my robe, I made my way into the kitchen. There was Sarge sitting at the table reading a newspaper. All I said was, "Coffee."

"I already poured you a cup, sit down and wake up. We have a long day ahead."

"Please Sarge, not now. I can't think until the affects of caffeine kick in," I mumbled.

While sitting there slowly coming to life, the phone rang. Sarge answered it on the second ring and started talking to Fred.

Seems Fred was on his way over in an hour to pick us up and drop us off at the train station. He told Sarge he was at the bagel shop and did we want anything? "Sure," Sarge replied, "I'll have my usual. Taylor, egg and cheese on an everything." Turning to me, he raised his eyebrows in a way that asked without a word. "Just a poppy with light cream cheese, thanks."

Coming out of my stupor, I headed to shower and got ready to leave. Sarge said he would take Lucey out. Last I saw her she moved up to my pillow and was still unconscious. Lucky dog.

Fred came in all perky; I knew I didn't like him for some reason, that might have been it. Anyway, we scarfed down our bagels and Fred went and checked in with the night officer.

We loaded our luggage in the van, took Lucey and left. Next stop was Penn Station in Newark. I sat in the back with Lucey, Sarge and Fred was up front. Traffic was light this ungodly hour in the morning. Then I noticed that Sarge became quiet and bent over. "Hey, are you alright? What's the matter? Fred what's with Sarge?"

"Sarge answered softly, "I think I'm going to be sick, Yia. All of a sudden I feel lightheaded and have bad belly cramps. You better let Fred take my place on the train while I get to a hospital."

"No Way Jose, I'll stay with you," I didn't like how this was going, it seemed to play into Fred's hands.

"Let me get examined at the ER Yia and if it's nothing I can catch up with you in Chicago. The plane is only an hour's ride. Please, I would be more comfortable knowing you were safe."

"Ok, but if there's a problem I'm coming back. I'm a nurse you know."

Lucey, Yeah, Florence Nightingale and she were in the same class.

"Just stay with the plan we made. I'll get checked out and call as soon as I can. Ok?"

"Ok."

Lucey, Oh No!

#17

Fred

I called ahead and got the bagel order from Sarge. I added a little extra something to Sarge's bagel and went to pick them up. I checked in with the night cop and he reported no activity. Good.

Onward, I found everyone including that mutt, ready to leave after some breakfast. I loaded their luggage in the van and off we went. Almost there the Sarge started to feel sick and needed to get medical attention. He told me to take care of Yia and drop him at a hospital or Urgent Center. Yia Yia was concerned and wanted to stay with him but luckily Sarge convinced to go on without him. Whew!

Calling ahead I had a patrol car ready to escort him to the nearest Emergency Room. I'm sure he'll be fine, just a little bellyache from that bagel. If I didn't need the money so much I don't think I could have gone through with this.

When we got to Penn Station, I put Sarge in the cop car and then took Yia Yia and that mutt into a private waiting room. Yia Yia was fretting about Sarge. The way she was carrying on, I suppose they are a lot closer than I thought. "He'll be fine, Yia. Good to get check though. I'll take you to Chicago and there we have a few hours layover until the next train. You can make your plans then no hurry until you know all the facts."

"Thanks Fred, I just feel terrible about leaving him. I suppose you're right, no sense for him to have me fussing. How long before we get on the train?" "Soon Yia, soon."

Amazing the amount of activity there was at the station, lots of people rushing here and there. I saw Red Caps driving luggage carts with some people riding back from their destination. It sure was a beehive of action. That annoying dog, Lucey got curious about the noise and crowds and started barking.

Lucey; Help Me. Help me!

I told Yia to quiet her down; I didn't want any curious people checking us out. Bad enough that Yia's a handful I have to take care of the dog too. Well, for a day or so it's not too bad.

The porter came in and said we were all set; next he had a Red Cap take our luggage and us to our train. I just had my emergency over night bag. I didn't want to seem like I knew I was going. I told Yia that all detectives carry them. She was OK with that explanation. I'll say she doesn't miss much.

We got off the ride and on board the train, the Lake Shore Limited that was taking us to Chicago. In addition to our train there must have been fifteen to twenty trains all hissing and giving off steam, all in an under ground cavern with out any signs of daylight. It was a little boy's dream coming true surrounded with all these steel giants. Do kids still pay with trains?

Our compartments were side by side, each with it's own tiny bathroom. The sink was in cabinets next to the sliding door with a half a pane of glass and a screen for privacy. A small table with two chairs stood on the opposite side of the door next to a window, very compact. Usually when I ride train I just have a seat in the general population, but I've never traveled this far.

I checked in with Yia once she got settled. As I was there someone who called himself Jose came in and introduced himself.

Said he would be our porter and if we had any questions or needs that he was our man. Lucey went over to sniff him and the immediately rolled on her back for a tummy rub. Guess she liked what she smelled. Anyway, he offered to take her out for walks; of course I immediately agreed.

Jose, heh? I'll get him checked out.

Lucey, Just sniffed Jose, he's A-Okay

Chicago, here we come. I put a call thru to Rocco to tell him what time we were arriving and told him that there was a four-hour lay over between trains. By that time he should be able to talk to Yia and by then the Sarge could meet us if he was able. I was starting to worry myself. He did look awfully ashen and in pain when he left us. I was assured the stuff I put on his bagel would just cause be a stomachache and it was temporary.

#18

Lucey

If this doesn't beat all, now I'm on the biggest train I've ever seen. The thing is a giant, even snorts steams and down right scary. A fellow named Jose greeted us on boarding. He's short, wiry with a take- charge attitude, said this was his train car. Asked if we had any questions and said he was going to take care of Yia and me on our trip. He seems ok. Better than that jerk, Fred that brought us here.

I don't like Fred. To me he is trying to horn in on a free Vay Kay and usurping Yia's affection, always winking and blinking. Must be some sort of disorder. I'm really worried about the Sarge. He was all doubled over and pale as a sheet when we dropped him off. I hope he's going to be okay. Guess I just got used to him being around. Yia sure is mean to him when he is but I can tell she's all concerned. She didn't even want to go without him. Said if he is still no better by the time we get to Chicago she is going to turn around and come back.

I was really looking forward to visiting with my pal Shirley. I guess we can postpone it. Somehow I feel that Fred is responsible for this whole situation. I better stick really close to Yia.

You never know what Fred has up his sleeve. No Siree Bob! I'm appointing myself her guard dog. I'm sharpening my bite. Too bad Yia had those teeth removed from me last year. I'll just have to gum him if necessary.

We got settled into our cabin. Boy this place is small. I immediately jumped on the bed and scratched myself a good resting place. Yia was fussing with her bag, getting out all kinds of stuff to push back aging. Wrinkle creams, hair spray, hair shine, mega vitamins, lots lotion, hands, face, body to smooth bumpy (creped) skin, breath freshener and lots other miscellaneous products that if she stopped using them I would go blind.

Don't picture it, not a pretty sight.

An "All aboard," rang out and this mammoth monster emitted a gigantic hiss of steam and started rolling out of the station. We traveled through a tunnel for a while then somewhere it emerged into daylight and went north along the Hudson River. Yia stared transfixed out the window. I think her thoughts were elsewhere. I went over to get a pet. She reached down and scratched behind my ear with nary a word. I hate to see her so quiet. It's not her style. Nope this is a sad, sad day for us!

#19

Yia

Lucey seems to feel my distress. Honestly, I think I should have stayed with Sarge. My heart is not in going. I promised myself that I would go back how if Sarge can't make it. It just doesn't seem right without him, farts and all.

Fred's ok, a bit full of himself but I'm sure he will protect me. Can you imagine at my age running from danger? It's surreal. I should be home knitting and cooking. Well, not so much knitting, I don't know how, but I succeed in the kitchen. I love making stuff for the Grands. Where else can you get kourambiedes, the Greek sugar cookies? The boys especially love them and I can tell where they have been by the powdered sugar trail they leave behind. Oh hopefully all will clear up and I can resume my Yia Yia duties including cooking and being a sex idol for the senior crowd.

We boarded the train and now I am staring out the window at the Hudson River; most of the foliage had dropped and I can see further into the scenery. Lucey has been quiet. I would have left her behind but I know she misses Shirley too. I sure hope Sarge gets better and resumes this journey. I asked Jose if I can get phone service on the train and he assured me I could. I'll wait a little while and give Sarge a call. I was hoping he would call me but how long can I wait?

I've never had much patience. Maybe I should pray for some. It would ease this worry.

"Oh patience where are you?"

Lucey: Oh no! Now I'm Patience again? What ever happed to Penance?

"Could this be my penance?"

Lucey: Well here's Penance, I'm just missing Strength

"Lord, give me strength!"

Lucey: Trifecta!

Soon it should be time for dinner, I was told already to dine in my room. Jose just dropped off the menu and I don't know whether or not to have Fred join me. It might cheer me up. It sure was convenient for him to be with us when Sarge took ill. Maybe a little too convenient, uh oh I am getting to see bad guys all over. I should be grateful instead of so suspicious.

#20

Fred

We got on the train and immediately this little twerp; Jose came over and asserted his authority. Well I showed him my badge and opened my jacket so he could catch a glimpse of my gun. When Yia went in her cabin, I let him know that she was in my protective custody and any communication with her had to go through me.

Had to get that pecking order in place right away. Jose might be in charge of the train but I'm in charge of Yia Yia and that mutt. I don't need a third party's interference. Bad enough I am uncomfortable about this situation without more stress. Yia's a loose cannon and that dog is no picnic either.

I'll be glad when this is over and I can get back, take care of some debts and the Sarge can worry about them. As soon as I got into my cabin I called Rocco on a throw away phone. Rocco informed me that he was already in Chicago with some of the Chicago Biker Boys. Said that he that would meet me at the hospitality room where the passengers wait for the next train. I asked about how he intended to talk Yia and he told me that when we got there that I should excuse myself to go to the restroom and he was going to ask Yia to step outside for some quiet conversation.

Again he assured me that she was in no danger from him. No, they just wanted to ask her some questions. My payoff was contingent on her being there and me taking a break. Of course, I assured him we were on our way and schedule to arrive around ten AM Central time. About my money, I was going to get it when I returned home.

Ok, this seemed almost too easy. One way or the other I was doing a round trip. A little of my conscience bothered me but now the plan was in action and all I had to do was excuse myself for a few minutes and wait for them to return Yia Yia. Actually, I'm not that bothered; she never even fell for my charms and has that annoying dog to boot.

Just as I hung up Jose knocked on my door with the room service menu, I told him I would order for Yia and my self in a few minutes. "No prob, Boss, I'll be back in a few." Well, at least he knows I'm the boss now, glad I straightened him out promptly.

I looked it over and went to Yia's cabin to get her order. We can have supper together and talk about tomorrow. As I left my room I went to see her only to realize she was at the Porter's station talking it up with Jose. She is maddening; how Sarge deals I have no idea.

"Yia, let's go back to your room and decide on supper," I was trying my best not to yell.

"No, that's Ok Fred, I just told Jose what I want and asked about when he planned to take Lucey for a walk."

"Let's go back to your cabin and discuss a few things, Yia," my frustration with her was mounting.

"You go ahead Fred I'll be there in a few," and she dismissed me, dismissed me in front of that pompous Jose. How humiliating, I could see him smirking at me.

All my hard work to protect her was going down the drain; I

looked foolish in front of Jose. I was beginning to feel sorry for Sarge.

Maybe it's time for her to get a good scare so she will cooperate.

I ordered my supper and chose to eat alone in my room, having enough of Yia and that dog for one day. I told Jose to serve Yia in her cabin and that I had some paper work to catch up on. I'll check our arrival time and call Rocco with the information. I'm hoping to get a good night's sleep; the clicky clack is annoying me too. Just wish tomorrow was over. Maybe I should give Sarge a call to see how he is; he should be fine by now.

No answer on his cell, guess that means he's busy or left it somewhere. No news is good news.

I realized Yia returned to her cabin so I went in to see her and get some plans made, hopefully she'll co-operate. I wanted her to make sure her cell was charged and remembered to close the curtain and lock her door. I will call her in the AM once I check the corridor and make sure it is clear. I told her to have her breakfast in her cabin and be prepared to leave when I come to get her. Definitely should arrive by 10 AM with a four-hour layover for the next train. That is if the Sarge is Ok. I left a message for him to call either way. I sure hope he comes I don't want to babysit her and that dog anymore.

I'm a little nervous about the Sarge arriving before Yia is back. Might be hard to explain. Think I'll call Rocco and make sure he's waiting for us. No sense in delaying Yia's return. It still amazes me how she can be the center of all this drama, she must have been a doozy in her day; she's sure a handful now.

#21
Yia

I saw Jose in the hall and left my cabin to have a word with him. Lucey was getting antsy and needed a walk. Jose told me he was coming to drop off tonight's supper menu and that we should be rolling into a next station in a few minutes. We were chatting it up and Jose mentioned that he just got out of the army. He was a training sergeant and lives upstate New York with his wife and teenage sons. I certainly could picture him as a drill sergeant. He was a no nonsense sort of guy.

While we were talking Fred came over with his shorts in a bunch because I wasn't in my room. I sent him on his way but I could hear mumbles under his breath when he left. What's his problem? Boy, I wish I could get a hold of Sarge, how much of this is a poor old lady suppose to take?

When I returned to my cabin, Fred came over and gave me his plans for the morning, Yadda, Yadda. Ok I'll try my best behaving as he wants even though it's cramping my free spirit. Good thing he never married, what a pain.

Calling the Sarge has me concerned, he isn't answering so I don't know if I'm headed back home or onward to Shirley. I'll know more in the morning I suppose. Jose came in with my supper; which wasn't bad, a cheap half bottle of wine and I was all set. He took Lucey and when he came back he cleaned up my supper dishes and then proceeded to get the berth ready for sleep. He was curious why I was in the protection program and I told him just the basic facts, no sense in talking too much.

As long as Lucey gave him the green light, I was comfortable with him around. Again I called the Sarge and again it went straight to voice mail. Now I am really starting to worry. Oh why did I leave him? I should have stayed an extra day to make sure he was ok. Tomorrow if I can't reach him I will buy a ticket back with or without Fred. Sarge probably needs my superior nursing skills, that and some good homemade chicken soup.

Well, I'll sleep fast and when I wake we should almost be in the windy city, Chicago. I would take a plane home but I don't want Lucey in the cargo area, she's crazy enough already without getting traumatized. Nope, plan B is on the table. It's all up to whatever news awaits.

Surprisingly, I fell asleep fast and didn't wake until the little peaks of sun rays sneaked in between the blind slats. It's looking to be a sun shiny day so far. I reached for my cell and tried once again to get hold of Sarge. Still no answer, my anxiety was reaching the outer limits. I looked over at Lucey who was all comfy cozy curled up on the foot of my berth. Somehow she managed to get herself all entangled in a blanket and was snoozing away.

I took a quick trip to the miniscule bathroom and then an even faster shower in that contraption, you have to shut the bathroom door tight and then turn on the water. Depending on your mood you can even sit on the toilet as you scrub away. Hard to describe, take my word for it.

I finished up putting myself together and was in need of a cuppa, luckily my friend Jose was already at his post. Ah, the first jolt of caffeine in the morning to start the day. While I was enjoying the brew my guardian, Fred came out of his cabin loaded for bear. He was all but snorting that I was supposed to be in my cabin awaiting him. Can I help it I'm a coffee junkie?

Keeping my mouth shut, I returned to my room while Lucey arose and stretched. Hearing Fred admonish me again was not pleasing her doggie mood. He'd better watch out, she'd probably gum him soon. Again I was reminded to stay away from the other passengers and Jose. We should be getting off this train and going to the station to wait for the next train.

If I don't reach Sarge I'm insisting on returning home, I can't travel with Fred any longer and my worry meter is working overtime.

Jose came in with my breakfast order and told me that some other workers were retuning to New York on an employee train and would be glad to accompany me if I wished. Good, I had another plan in place.

We were set to arrive in Chicago in 15 minutes and then onward to the hospitality room. Jose secured a Red Cap that was taking luggage and some passengers. So Lucey, Fred and I rode this baggage chariot into the station and were deposited at a large waiting room. Our luggage was tagged and placed in a room and we were free to roam around if we wished. Being we had over 4 hours to wait I wanted to go outside and see the city. Of course that got shot down right away by you know who!

One more time I attempted to reach Sarge. If I don't hear from him in a couple of hours I plan to get a ticket back to New York. Fred was trying to reach him too, he's so jittery this morning, maybe he didn't sleep well.

Making myself comfortable in one of the big overstuffed chairs and I started to read the Chicago Tribune; it's the city's daily paper for the area. Fred told me to stay put that he had to run to the men's room for a minute. So that's it, he has a stomachache. I knew something was wrong. He left and I become totally engrossed in the paper I was suddenly interrupted by of all people, Rocco, he's one of the Motorcycle Club's member.

"Hey Rocco, how are you, how's the gang?"

" Well, Yia you know that some of our members had to do sometime in the Big House after you ratted them out. I'm surprised at you. Never took you for a snitch."

"Oh Rocco, that's just not me, no it was Lucey my dog, she had some kind of special cookie that transmitted info to the cops, I love you guys. "

"Well, Yia, I was sure there was an explanation to all of this. Why don't you come with me for a minute and tell it to Turk. He just got out and wants to talk to you."

"Gee, you know Rocco, I was wondering how you knew I was here."

"Yia, I just go where the Turk tells me. He told me we were going to Chicago and I was to come in here and take you out to talk to him."

" Well, just seems a little strange to me, nobody is supposed to know where I am. Hmm, ok I'll take a chance but I have to be back soon, I have this cop that is watching my every move, he just went to the bathroom so let's make it quick."

Lucey was reluctant, she never like my motorcycle friends. She was not coming along easily. Rocco said just leave her, we'd be right back.

Good enough, Fred can watch her for a few minutes. I grabbed my purse and followed Rocco out the door.

Going through the doorway there was two burly looking guys waiting when I came out they both grabbed me by the elbows and lifted me off the ground. Uh oh, this can't be good. I started kicking the air and was going to yell before the guy on my left showed me his knife and suggested I keep quiet.

Just then I spotted Jose coming towards me with another porter, I mouthed, "Help me!" then Lucey arrived and started biting the guy to my right. Jose rushed into the fray with his friend and I was dropped like a sack of potatoes. Pretty soon the security men came over and broke up the fight but not before Rocco got away.

As things were settling down I looked up and standing there was the Sarge struggling with Rocco.

Boy was I ever glad to see him. He looked a little tired but he sure was a sight for these sore eyes.

#22
Sarge

My brief stay in the hospital was medieval. I felt horrible when I arrived and was quickly ushered into an exam room. The patrol officer that brought me stayed close and I was glad I had someone there; I was all weak and shaky and just feeling awful.

When the Doctor came in I got a quick exam, some blood taken and an IV started right away. It was determined that whatever was going on as caused by the bagel I wolfed down. I was given some kind of liquid medicine that made me throw up and when that was over then a stomach tube was passed to wash out whatever was left. I swear all this happened in 20 minutes. In the next 10 minutes I began feeling so much better. I asked the Doctor what it was but he said some of the stomach contents were sent to the lab for id. On a guess he thought I was poisoned.

Wow, that was a shocker, I couldn't think clearly as to who or why. My next thoughts turned to Yia Yia and I was afraid she was in imminent danger. I grabbed my jacket looking for my cell phone but it wasn't there. I checked all my other pockets with no luck. The only place it could be was in the car. It must have fell out my pocket without me realizing it.

I asked the cop who was with me if he knew Fred's number, but no, so I borrowed his phone and called my station. Finally getting Fred's mobile number I started calling him. Then I re-thought the situation and decided to wait for the lab results to come back. Yia was safe on the train and I had time to get all the facts right.

Feeling stronger by the minute I asked to be release, the good Doctor who looked like a boy scout said to wait for another hour, by that time he would know what the causative agent was and also give me a chance to rest and get better. Okay, I could do that.

Jack, my cop savior said he had to write up a report and would be back in an hour. I thanked him profusely and felt the benefits of being in the brotherhood.

Upon being released, Jack returned and took me to the air-port, he talked to someone and before I knew it I was on a plane going to O'Hare's airport in Chicago. On landing I took a cab to the hotel nearest the train station and spent the rest of the day just relaxing and catching up with sleep. I never realized how tired one could get. Next morning I checked out and cabbed to the train station, I timed it so I could be there before Yia's train pulled in.

I paid the cabbie and headed to the front door when I saw and then realized that the Turk was standing there, strange. It wasn't but a moment when one of his men bounded through the door. Approaching them, I saw Turk having an animated conversation with his henchmen, Rocco.

They were busy talking as I neared, then Turk spotted me and ran off, leaving Rocco who turned and saw me and started to run. Luckily I grabbed him and dragged him back into the station. He was saying he didn't do nuthin, "So why did you run?" His reply was that he didn't know, in fact he said it again he didn't know "nuthin."

Once inside I noticed a ruckus going on a few feet away. It seems that security and a couple of porters had two men subdued while Yia Yia was bashing them with her pocketbook. Can't that woman stay out of trouble?

I rushed over and interrupted the pocketbook bashing and asked what was the problem was. Yia answered that Rocco, who I held by the nape of his neck and the two she was hitting tried to kidnap her. Rocco again said, "I know nuthin." I asked where Fred was and she said he went to the men's room and that Rocco approached her and said that Turk wanted to have a few words with her. She said she went willingly until these two characters grabbed her and was whisking her to the door. She said she was saved by Jose and Carlos, his friend, and co-worker who jumped into the fray.

Whew, a lot of info in a few minutes, but most of all she gave me the biggest hug ever and said she was so happy to see me. Told me she was going to come back to Jersey if I wasn't better and that Fred was a jerk.

Security took the three suspects back to their office where I was to join them with Yia to file a report; meanwhile I was trying to decide on how to handle Fred. Yia and I decided that I should just go into the hospitality room and sit in her chair with Lucey, it would be interesting to see what Fred would do. Okay, not much of a plan but doable.

I tied Lucey to a chair then sat down and made myself comfortable. It was a few minutes before Fred returned, he was startled to see me and then asked if I saw Yia Yia. "No, I thought you would know, you are in charge of her," I said. "Yeah but I had to use the facilities and told her to stay put, she never listens," was his prompt answer.

True that, she does manage to go off the grid sometimes but I had a feeling there was more to it than Fred wanted to say. Fred didn't seem that surprised to see me, asking how I was feeling. Next he was glad I could take over at this point.

"Maybe we should go look for her, she couldn't have gone far, Fred," I was checking for a reaction. He appeared calm and said she should be back in a couple of minutes, for me to relax. "I don't know Fred, aren't you a little worried, after all you're her protective agent?"

His reply was a mini confession. He told me that her friend Rocco from the motorcycle club approached him and told him that the head guy, the Turk, needed to speak to her for a few minutes. He was assured that she would be fine and for me not to worry.

"Fred, how can you be so naïve? I just walked in on two thugs struggling with her right after I grabbed Rocco as he bounded out of the station. Told him the Turk ran off when he saw me and Rocco was playing innocent. What else do you know Fred and let's start with what you added to my bagel."

Fred turned pale and started to sweat, admitted he added a little spread to my bagel that he got from Rocco and that the Turk promised no harm would come to Yia; just needed a little talk. "And how much were you going to get for your trouble Fred, must be something in it for you." I pressed.

Fred squirmed on that question but said he was not going to get anything if Yia didn't meet up with Turk and did I have to report this incidence to our superiors?

I really should report this but Fred has been a life long friend, he's been my partner and was there when my wife died. If Yia went willingly and no harm came to her, sort of put me between a rock and a hard place.

He almost killed me and put Yia Yia in a very dangerous situation. His actions could have been a disaster if those thugs succeeded.

Fred pleaded with me, said he would be brought up on charges and might lose his pension. Maybe, he said he got into the ponies a little but he meant Yia no harm and he would not deliberately harm me. I chose to believe him but told him that I had to think on it for a while.

Looking up I saw Yia walking across the room a little worse for wear but in good spirits.

I told Fred to beat it and I would handle Yia Yia. It didn't take much encouragement as he bounded away and practically knock over a few passengers. Talk about a man on a mission.

#23

Lucey

I wish I knew what the blazes was going on around here. Soon as we got off the train we were whisked into the hospitality room. Some hospitality, no dog treats or any other pooches around that I could impress.

Fred and Yia took chairs, I was tied to the leg of the chair that Yia sat in then Fred said something and he disappears, next comes that motorcycle creep, Rocco. He says something to Yia and off she disappears with him. I felt something was going on a ran off to be with Yia, What I saw next was her struggling with two brutes, I wasted no time in biting one of them in the ankle. Believe it or not in comes the Sarge struggling with one of the Biker Boys. He takes my leash, sends Yia with the security guys and goes and sits the chair Yia used. He bends down and gives me an ear scratch and waits for Fred.

Fred comes back, startled to see the Sarge. They had some words, and I could tell that Sarge was not too happy. Next thing I know is Fred takes off and then Yia shows back up. I'm getting dizzy from all the head turning. It's probably a whiplash, I need a steak or something.

From what I could hear, seems Fred is in some kind of trouble, Yia and Sarge talked about continuing on the trip to see Shirley. Sarge was all happy to see Yia and she was all happy to see him but neither one of them said anything about being happy to see me. I felt like an orphan.

They were so busy talking to each other speaking so quickly and hardly coming up for air that I was getting exhausted. Maybe I should nip Sarge's ankle and get some attention. Nah, I'll just get yelled at and feel humiliated.

At last they calmed down and I could understand what was happening. Seems Sarge is concerned that maybe some information either by Fred or some other leak that puts their trip in danger. Sarge told Yia about Fred's role in making him sick and when he confronted Fred, Sarge said he was sure that Fred really didn't mean to hurt him, just put him out of action for a while. That Fred was in some financial difficulties and some how the motorcycle gang found out and made him an offer including getting Sarge disabled.

Yia's head was bouncing up and down so fast she looked like one of those bobble head dolls. I was getting exhausted. Luckily Sarge didn't tell Fred their final destination.

Sage suggested that they get a light lunch, that he was starving. So off they went to one of the station's eateries. I had to pretend to be a therapy dog so I could get admitted. Therapy dog, I'm the one that needs therapy. All this excitement is too much for a sensitive pooch such as myself.

Honestly, I sure am glad that the Sarge is back. Fred is a no goodnik. Never even gave me a pet or an ear scratch. I should have bitten him just for good measure.

A couple of hours to wait before traveling on to see my pal Shirley; I sure do miss her. I wonder if she still eats dog milk bones. Just wondering.

#24
Yia

Sarge has been recuperating with a lot of down time in his cabin. Feeling confident I decided to explore the train. Of course there's the dining room that is open for breakfast, lunch and dinner, offering room service for the compartments. On to the observation car with almost panorama windows, it's great way to see the country. Going between the cars is a covered awning that joins the doors you go through to get from on car to the next. After that are the cars with just seats and of course the locomotive that I wasn't allowed to visit. How rude!

Yesterday we boarded the Empire Builder train late afternoon and I had dinner in my room. Sarge wasn't much into eating but he kept me company for a while and bid me an early, " Good Evening." He's still not himself, no rules or conditions or any instructions as to my conduct. He's really affected by this whole thing with Fred. Dispirited, I think. It's hard when you have faith in someone only to have him let you down.

We were traveling through Wisconsin but it was night and nothing but distant lights to see. The attendant came in took out the dinner trays and proceeded to make up my bed. Lucey had her last walk at the next depot and then it was time to sleep for both of us. After she rooted around looking for a spot to be all comfy cozy, I finally fell of and woke to bright sunshine pouring through the window blinds. The smell of coffee did the job of bringing me to life and when I got up and peered at the view we were in Minnesota. Not that I knew, it was what the nice attendant told me.

I asked if Sarge was awake yet and the attendant told me he was up and about and actually in the dining car right now. I debated whether or not to join him but thought better of it. He probably needs some alone time to get himself back on track. I'll spoil myself with a room service breakfast and get a lazy start to the day.

Looking out my window I could only see lots of pastures and an occasional house. Some much space here, not like the East Coast where some many people are all jammed together. I bet it gets lonely though.

Settling into the train's routine, I read for a while, looked out my window, finally got the nerve to get into that weird toilet/shower combo and was ready for? I'll figure that out later. I'll just go check on Sarge and cheer him up, no long faces today. The sun is shining and we are traveling cross-country. Is America great or what?

At the next stop I plan to stretch my legs and walk Lucey myself. No sense in getting too spoiled; plus I have to keep this girlish body in shape.

Just as I was putting on the last of my mascara (Can't live without that stuff) when Sarge knocked on my cabin door. He looked a lot better and was almost the same old bossy self. "Where do you think you're going all dressed up?" was his first question. "Well, Good Morning to you too, I see you're feeling better." Sorry, but I didn't need attitude after all that worrying I did on his behalf.

I told him I planned to walk Lucey and that was met with a "NO WAY" remark. Well, he's back to normal, giving me orders and being a pain. I got a lecture on having a false sense of security on this train and I was to be very cautious on where I went and to whom I spoke. How can I, a free spirit like myself deal with this?

Then I was treated to another lecture, which went in one ear and out the other. I can quote them chapter and verse and I'm sorry if Sarge sees shadows everywhere and I can't be my gregarious self. I was almost the Senior Citizen Sex Idol just a few months ago. I know he's just jealous, that has to be it. It's hard to be in charge of a celebrity such as myself. Ok I understand, I'll sacrificed a little a little freedom, after all we'll be in Oregon where I can't wait to see Shirley and breathe West Coast air. Not to speak of having a taste of all the wines, ok give a little to get a little.

Can't walk the dog, can't eat in the dining room at least not yet, no wandering around the train.(I didn't tell him I did already) and under no circumstances and I to start talking to strangers. Hey, they are all strangers here!

So there it is, I knew he had a bunch of rules for me, I'm a prisoner because of being too friendly. Drats!

#25

Lucey

You do understand that I am a mere 25 pounds, well, maybe a tad more but I am still a small pooch. I know have complained before of the chaotic life I lead with my owner. Actually, I thought it I had it made. She was on in years, a bit dull and I could lead a peaceful yet comfortable existence.

Far from it, even an axe murder has down time. First she has Shirley ride around the Town house property on an ironing board, then the neighbors has banned us from the clubhouse after her marching band cleaned out that clubhouse of anything that wasn't nailed down.

Add to that holding up a few banks thinking she was into getting dates for the felons on the motorcycles, next I had to spend time with Shirley at the Rehab Hospital, and had to be part of a patient's show. Lastly she runs around the neighborhood in a flesh colored body suit that winds up with her having to be in the witness protection program. Confused yet? Well, just imagine living it!

Right now I am a train speeding somewhere, it's not bad, I get plenty of walks and treats and at night I get to sleep while being gently rocked by the train's movements. It's just during the day that I deal with Yia Yia.

She was all concerned about Sarge and now they are both bickering again. There's no hope for them. She hasn't mentioned the mysterious box yet and neither has he. I was hoping it was a receipt for a doggie pal for me but no such luck. Last trip on the boat I met this poodle and I was sure was a distant relative. Explains my pouty lips and je ne sais pas, my French background. That boat trip ended in disaster too! I was required to spy on Yia again via nanolaced cookies that made everyone on the ship sick when Yia gave them to one of the room attendant's boyfriend chef. Again don't ask. A talent show that Yia almost won which had the Sarge shaking and ready to quit his protective duties.

So without going into more detail, my life span has been shortened by the frenetic escapes of this septuagenarian. We are supposed to visit Shirley and her Greek husband George on some vineyard in Oregon. I hope there is someone there that I can have some fun with. No mortal dangers or anything just some romping round and tugs of wars, burying bones. Normal stuff!

#26

Sarge

I'm starting to get my strength back. It is just so hard to wrap my head around what Fred tried to do. The Doctor at the hospital said that the poison I ingested was strong and it was a good thing I sort out medical attention immediately. I really don't think Fred meant to kill me, he was just duped into trying to get me out of the way for a little while. I didn't report any of this to my superiors, I'll take my time about it and maybe I won't have to be a narc. Fred and I go back a long way, it's like turning in your brother.

I made a promise to myself to be a little more patient with Yia Yia. The woman has so much energy and is so naïve in a lot of ways. Being away from her family is difficult I know, but she sure can be a handful sometimes.

Maybe we can get some relaxing in at George's vineyard. This mini vay-kay will give the authorities time to check out the location and intentions of the gang that wishes Yia harm.

I think I will invite Yia to have some lunch in the dining car and then after checking out the observation car, we can spend some time in there. So far this trip has been quiet, I hope it continues, you never know what kind of mischief Yia can cause.

It will be a couple more days until we reach our destinations. I'm sure the rest will do us both some good.

No suspicious characters on board and we've settled into the train's routine. Even Lucey has become bearable. With any luck the same will be said about Yia Yia soon. One could always hope.

Well, I'd better go see what today will bring, had myself enough excitement for a while.

#27

Lucey

There I was all snug and comfy wrapped up in the bed covers and snoozing away. Yia was in that miniature toilet/ shower combo getting a start on the day. Then a gentle rap on the door followed by an, "All-o Miss Yia Yia."

It was Rosita the room attendant; she's been taking me on my bathroom breaks for the past couple of days. It's unhealthy for someone to be so cheerful in the morning. Maybe if I ignore her she'll go away.

"Ah, there you are my little puppee! Come on, we go outside and you do some peepeee." "No, I have better idea, how about I tie a rope on your chubby leettle neck and drag you outside to make some peepeee?" Rosita is from Mexico, I think, and she is just too cheerful especially in the morning. It's disgraceful. She must eat too many tacos or burritos because her fanny is so what's the word? Oh yeah, mucho!" I'm trying my best to ignore her.

Yesterday she was quizzing Yia about where we are headed and what about that handsome man next cabin. Was he Yia's boyfriend? That's when Yia told her all about being in the witness protection program and how we were going to see her friend who lives out west and hide out for a while. Rosita's big brown eyes widen as she soaked up all this information. I don't think Sarge would like Yia blabbing so much to a stranger.

She said in her Spanish accent that Yia was such a character; how exciting her life was and on and on. Yia soaked it all up and played nonchalant. I'm getting more paranoid with aging, the Yia talks too much.

Now Rosita shouts to Yia who was still in the bathroom and told her the train was pulling into a station and she was taking me out for my walk. An 'Okey Dokey' emitted from Yia and I was hooked up to my leash and pulled out of my nice warm bed.

All these stations look the same to me and all have a pet place for dogs traveling with their family. Rosita was in a big rush this morning and before returning the train she ran over to the pay phone. I don't know who she was talking to but she told the person on the listening end that she had some good information about a passenger who is in the witness protection program and it was going to cost them some big bucks for the information. Yikes, you know what that means? She's narcing on Yia and putting me in danger. I sure wish I could speak English sometimes, this being one of them. What a rat! All sweet and nice to Yia and informing on her behind her back: I should bite Rosita in her ankle or something. I was tugging and pulling on my leash to get her off the phone but she just kept yapping away.

Just when I thought I'd get some R&R and romp around with Shirley, I will have to be on guard duty again. Is there no justice?

#28

Sarge

I was just getting ready to go for breakfast when I looked out my train window and saw Rosita the attendant on a pay phone. It did strike me as being odd and then I saw Lucey tugging her and straining at her leash. Rosita kept yanking her back and at one time gave Lucey a smack on her backside to make her stop. Something's not right here. I got a sinking feeling and decided see Yia. I am sure she knows something about something.

I knocked on her cabin door and she opened it not expecting me. "Oh, Hi Sarge, I thought it was Rosita bringing Lucey back." I told her I needed to ask her a couple of questions and she said, "Sure, what's up?"

I didn't waste anytime; right off I asked her if Rosita knew she was in the witness protection program. Her hesitation told me all I needed to know. "What did you tell her, Yia and when?"

After a couple of ums and gees, she admitted that she happened to mention that she was being protected by me, of course that's after Rosita was curious about my being next door and of course how attractive I was. "Can't you see Yia, she set you up." "Don't be ridiculous, you see bad guys all over. She's a hard working woman who was just curious, that's all, we had some girl talk. She's got a young family in Mexico and her husband is in the army. Her Mom takes care of the children while she works. How can you think she's involved with the baddies after me?"

"Because Yia, I am here to protect you and keep you safe, you telling someone your situation, no matter whoever they are, puts us both in danger." I could tell that Yia was not taking this seriously. I wanted to tell her about seeing her on the pay phone and her being mean to Lucey but decided that I was going to make changes without Yia's knowledge. She just managed to put us both in danger. This is what I mean about her being so naïve and trusting.

As we were talking Rosita brought Lucey back, who was not happy. She greeted me and then softly growled at Rosita. Yia was shocked, said Lucey never growled, well hardly ever. She started to admonish the dog but I just said the she is having a hard time with all the adjusting she has been doing. Rosita and Yia bought that as Lucey jumped back on the bed with a stance of a German Shepard. She's a real spunky little dog. I bet she would tell all if she could speak English. Maybe I can learn dog speak and get some info from her. Later, I'll try later. Meanwhile, after Rosita left I told Yia we better have breakfast in our rooms. I didn't want her in the dining hall or anywhere public until I came up with a plan.

Of course Yia thought I was being over protective and was cranky. Well better safe and cranky then in harms way. I ordered some breakfast for us both with some extra bacon to slip to Lucey. Yia was telling me I see danger every place I look and how can I be so untrusting of everyone. I was trying hard to ignore her but she was really getting under my skin.

"Enough Yia, I am trying to protect you and that dog of yours along with my own hide. I'm trying to think of what to do next to insure our safety so just stick a sock in it!" My little tantrum quieted her down for a minute and Lucey gave me a paws up sign, I think. I'd better call the chief and bring him up to speed with what has happened. I leave it to him to decide our next move.

Here we are somewhere in the mid west and I have no clue on what to expect next. My gut tells me to get off this train but I have no idea if Rosita knows our final destination. I'll have to make peace with Yia and then go out and see if the train workers know our route.

After our unpleasant breakfast, I went out to the conductor who is charge of our train car. His name is Jose, a short scrappy fellow who was in the US Army. I recognized him as one of the fellows that in the fray at the Chicago station. I thanked him for helping save the day for Yia and me. "No problem, you were outnumbered, just wanted to even the score." "Well, you did and thanks again." I said. Then I asked if he knew of our special circumstances and he gave me a suspicious look and asked for my ID. I liked his style. Anyway, once he verified I was who I said I was he asked me why I wanted to know. Very cautious fellow; would have made a good cop.

Jose told me he was the conductor on the Lake Shore Limited that brought Yia and her protecter to Chicago. Said he didn't care for Fred. He was asserted his authority over her, which she promptly ignored. Jose said he could tell Yia Yia was very worried about someone and tried her best to keep up a friendly front. "Funny thing, you know, I get a sixth sense about the people on my train. She's a handful but a good person, Fred, not so much. I'm glad you took over. She's much more relaxed."

I leveled with him and told him that my witness had confided to the cabin attendant that she was in my protective custody and in the protection program. Jose listened, said he knew of my special circumstances but it was not for anyone else's information. When I asked if the room attendant had access to our destination, he replied she did. All the train tickets were available to the workers on the train car.

Not good, a bad feeling came over me and I had to check in with my boss to get some guidance. Now I was truly mad at Yia for putting us in the situation. See what I mean about her being so naïve? I thanked Jose and told him I would take it from there. He just shook his head and said, "Women."

Back in my cabin I reached out to my boss and explain the breach in our plans. He told me to sit tight and he would get back to me in a few.

Meanwhile, I confined Yia to her cabin and was subjected to a long, icy stare. Hey, I didn't talk too much, why is she mad at me?

A little later my cell phone rang and it was my boss. He said that we were to get off the train at the next stop. Under no circumstances were we to tell anyone anything!! He reserved a car for us and two disguises for me and Yia. I was to give him our sizes and he would do the rest. Next we were to drive to the nearest airport that would be in Grand Forks, North Dakota, not far from the train station. Arriving there we will be met by a Federal agent who would give us our clothes and take us to our plane. I was to be a Pilot hitching a ride along with Yia dressed as a stewardess. I don't know if he knows how old she is but I didn't want to make waves.

#29

Jose

I have been a conductor for Amtrak going on 6 years now. As soon as my 20 years was up I left the US Army. It was a hard life for my family going from post to post, especially the kids; two, two boys getting to be teenagers now and need a tougher hand.

When discharged, I bought a little home about 100 miles north of New York City. It's semi-rural. Has a good high school and the property needs enough work for two active teenagers to keep them out of trouble .I didn't want them growing up on the streets with time on their hands. I'm lucky to have found a good woman who agrees to this plan. Mostly!

I travel each week from the East Coast to the West Coast and the turn around and head back. Two weeks on and two weeks off; it's been working out okay. My wife is used to longer absences and the boys are more responsible with the chores that are needed.

I've met some interesting people in the past few years but this trip is like the best of the bunch.

I get notified in New York that I will have a witness and a protector on board on the way to Chicago. I expect an Al Capone or some kind of wise guy, but no. A sweet little old lady and a very macho twit arrive. He makes no time in trying to show me whose boss. Gave me a glimpse of his puny gun. A lot of rules and dos and don't to go along with them, Well, the sweet little old lady,

Yia, paid no attention to him which drove him to distraction. Came out for a chat and her first morning coffee. I liked her and couldn't imagine why she was in protective custody. I could tell she was worried about something or someone and she was about to tell me when her bodyguard interfered.

When we arrived in Chicago we had a 4-hour lay over, then I switch to the Empire Builder for the long journey to the West. Having the time, I left the station and met up with a few co-workers for a walk around the Windy City. On the way back into the station I see two burly guys each holding Yia Yia up by her elbows. I spot her and she mouths, "Help me!! Help me!"

Well, me and my friends run over and pull them off her then security gets into the game and another guy comes in dragging a goon with him; Yia and her assailants go off to the security office and this fellow, Sarge introduces himself to me. Seems he was to be her protector and got sick, he is here now to continue the journey.

My head is spinning with all the information but I have to go to the Security office to file a report, I'll get the rest later. She has to be some kind of woman. What could she have done? She looks like she's just a sweet old lady. Hey, you never know.

When I got on the Empire Builder, I had the train segment with the individual staterooms. Being it was my lucky day; I had the two of them, the witness and her protector. Here I thought it was going to be an easy trip.

Once boarded the guy, Sarge came out and gave me some information. Seems the sweet old lady tiffed off some really bad characters. If it wasn't for me and my friends she might have been harmed. He wanted to thank me for intervening. You know, he's okay.

He said everyone called him Sarge and that if I had any suggestions or ideas I knew where to find him. Also told me that although Yia look a little old and sweet not to be taken in by her, it wasn't an act, it was she had a way of getting into trouble.

I told him I would bear that in mind and wished him an easy trip, I hoped he got to relax, he looked a little shaky.

My helper, Rosita was busy getting everyone comfortable and I thought I would keep the information Sarge gave me to myself. She's a good woman but I think I'm not ready to share. Not yet at least.

Yia left her room and saw me. Thanked me again for helping her and said she was happy I was on the journey west with her.

Next morning, closer to noon, Sarge comes out to speak to me.

Seems the little old lady, Yia, blew their cover. She told Rosita, the attendant that she was in the witness program and that Sarge wasn't her boyfriend but a cop. Now the Sarge is in a dilemma. He said he called his superior and he has to get off the train at the Grand Forks station. Did I know it? I replied it was a big station and close to an airport. Asked if I could reassign Rosita to another train segment, no problem for me. Then he said he didn't want anyone to know that he and Yia Yia were leaving the train and asked me to cover for him; a lot of cloak and daggers going on here. I thought to myself that Yia really must be in danger for all the subterfuge going on. Anyway, I told him that whatever he needed I was his man.

#30

Yia

I was getting ready to go to lunch when Sarge knocked on my cabin door. I thought he was going to join me but no! Seems my telling Rosita about my problems brought out the paranoid Sarge and he has made arrangements for us to leave the train and get west via a plane. No way!! I hate to fly, I haven't been on a plane in ages and don't want to go now. Then there's Lucey, I'm not putting her in the baggage compartment, she's crazy now just imagine her worse. Nope, count me out.

He sat down and explained the situation to me and reluctantly I agreed to go on the condition that Lucey stays with me, no cargo area for her. He said we could make her a therapy dog. Actually, she could use some therapy but I don't think he meant that.

He was going to ride up front dressed as a pilot hitching a ride and I was to sit in the back as a stewardess. Well, I'll try it but it's going to take some nerve pills to get me on that flying contraption. Next stop we leave the train and meet up with an agent. He'll have out uniforms. Sarge needed to know my size. Really? My dress size isn't too bad but my shoe size is gnormous.

He, the Sarge hasn't said much about Fred. All I got was that he was in a hurry to get back to New Jersey and told Sarge to say 'Good-bye' to me. Fine by me, he was a real pain and I'm glad the

Sarge is back, at times anyway.

If I didn't want to visit with Shirley I don't think I'd be going through all this cloak and dagger routine. I asked what was our destination on the plane and Sarge said he wouldn't tell me because I talk too much. Really?

Next he told me just to pack an over night bag and that our luggage would be sent to us when we reached our destination. I need one bag just for all my vitamins and cosmetics. How else can I keep this girlish figure and the wrinkles at bay? Good Lord, I started praying for patience and then Lucey started annoying me. What a day!

Lucey, Patience. Patience!! Guess that's my name of the day!! Good Lord!!

#31

Jose

I rotated Rosita to another car and hope my new attendant knows how to keep the passenger's confidences. Just a few more hours until we reach Grand Forks station. According to Sarge, he will be detraining and meeting with an agent. Too bad their journey is interrupted by one of our employees. I can see he is concerned for Yia's safety and takes his job seriously; just hated the interruption to be caused by our staff.

I gave Sarge my home number and told him to stay in touch, I hope he does; he was okay in my book. I can see he has his hands full with the older lady. She certainly kept him busy.

Anyway the plan is to keep the charade going that they are both in their cabins. I will take care of that as long as possible. That will give them some time to get away secretly.

I wished him good luck and told him I would do whatever he needed. Sure hope he manages to reel in Yia, that's his biggest obstacle.

As I was finishing up some paper work, Sarge came out of his cabin. He told me that they were leaving their luggage behind and is there a way I can forward their bags? I told him we do it all the time and just make sure that they are labeled and to give me the address where he wanted them sent. He tried slipping me some cash, I declined and said I'd send him the bill for the luggage later and I was sorry he couldn't complete his journey on the train. He's OK in my book. Reminds me of some of my guys in my Army outfit. To the point and is a hundred percent on the job. Not too many of us like that anymore.

In a few more hours we will be in Grand Forks, North Dakota. It's a fairly large station and close to the airport. Sarge plans to get off the train at Grand Forks. He will appear to be just stretching his and Yia's legs and walking the dog, but will not get back on the train. I wished him all good luck and reminded him to keep in touch.

#32
Lucey

Hey!! I was sleeping all comfy cozy, wrapped up and snuggled on the berth. I was in a hair's breath of catching a perfectly grilled pork chop when Yia Yia rudely interrupted my dream. What's up with that?

She said it was time for my walk but when I looked through the slats on the window it was still pitch black outside. I'm telling you kids, she is losing it. Next thing I know I have my leash on and she's yanking me from my warm bed. There should be a law!

As I let go of my dream and stretched, a gentle knock came on the door, it was (who else?) Sarge. He was all dressed and raring to go. What's up with these two? Always something. I was just getting the hang of this train stuff except for Rosita. She spanked me and was transferred, so once again I was a happy camper.

Yia let Sarge in and then another knock followed and in came Jose. He brought some breakfast stuff, coffee, muffin and fruit. As you can tell there was no pork chop or food for me. Another black mark for him, I'm keeping score.

After the morning chatter died down I overheard their plan. We were to get off the train, walk around the station and connect with an agent who will then give them their disguises. Sarge is to be an airplane pilot and Yia stewardess. Really? A stewardess? Do these guys have any idea how old this person is? It's a bit of a stretch, but what do I know? They must be hard up for staff. Stewardess.

There wasn't any mention on how I was to get on the plane. I'm already a therapy dog. It would seem a pilot or stewardess wouldn't need therapy. Right? Actually they probably are a bunch of whackos to begin with, but why advertise? Then I heard my fate. A little crate that they plan to stuff me into and then carry it on board. A loss of personal freedom; I am sure I could be a comfort to a panicky passenger. This plan doesn't work for me. Don't I get a vote?

I jumped back on the berth as they were chatting away. Why waste a perfectly good opportunity to catch some ZZZ's. It wasn't to last, the breakfast club broke up, Jose left after a lot of back slapping and keep in touch stuff. Next thing I know the train enters a station and I am once again yanked from my pursuit of my dream pork chop. Later....

#33

Jose

When breakfast was finished, Sarge and Yia were ready to roll but Yia's dog, Lucey was all curled up under the covers and had to be coaxed off the bed. Yia tempted her with some leftover muffin but Lucey had something different in mind. She sure was a cute if not a fussy kind of dog.

When the train pulled into the station, we waited until everyone detrained, then the Sarge, Yia and dog Lucey left. I was sorry they had to leave. Sarge was my kind of guy and we were deep into forming a nice friendship when he parted. I promised to do my best to keep up the appearance that they were still aboard. It will give them some time to get away and cover their tracks.

I watched as they departed, Sarge was very differential to the old girl, I think he had a soft spot for her. Goodness knows she definitely a handful. That dog of hers is no picnic either. I saw them walk down the station platform until they were out of sight. Really, what could she have done? Somebody bad wants to seek revenge, I'm glad I could help. I felt responsible for Rosita blowing their cover albeit it was Yia who took Rosita into her confidence. What's done is done, hopefully it will turn out ok.

I busied myself with the morning routines. Took their luggage to the place to be sent on and got ready for the next leg of the trip. Life moves on and I can't wait for the return trip home. My sons are giving their Mom the normal teenage stuff. They need me home more. I think I'll ask for no more long voyages. Couple of days away at most, besides I'm not getting any younger myself.

Sarge promised he'd get in touch when things get back to normal. I personally think that it may be a while. Que sera, sera!!

#34

Sarge

Well, we were all set to leave the train, I had a small back pack as did Yia. Lucey for some reason was reluctant to leave the comfort of the berth, guess she was getting used to train living I had to drag and coax her. Yia and I with the dog in tow walked the length of the station. The train was hissing and letting off steam ready for the rest of the journey West. I was on the look out for our contact, who was to bring us to the airport.

I was searching the parking lot as we neared the end of the walkway, then I spotted a flash of headlights. When I looked again, the car lights flashed again. That must be my connection. I hurried Yia and Lucey then approached the car. The driver to my surprise was a woman. She introduced herself as Agent Smith and told me she had our outfits ready. We got in the back seat with Lucey as she drove us to the airport. I asked her about our destination and she handed me some papers.

Yia was desperately trying to read them the same time as me, Lucey was more interested in the Agent's lunch. We were to travel to San Francisco and meet up with another agent there who was going to rent us a car for the final lap of our journey.

We were given our clothing and Agent Smith suggested we change in the car before we left.. I was a little shy to strip to my underwear with Yia in the car so we agreed to take turns. Me first,

I had a spiffy pilots suit, wings to match and shiny black shoes. My ID was Captain Brown and I was going to sit up front with the real pilots for the two hour trip. All set it was Yia's turn and she was given a stewardess uniform, She made sure our backs were turned as she donned the outfit. It was a pantsuit in navy blue with matching loafers. I must admit she looked pretty nice. She was just to sit in the back with the other stewardesses and try to mind her own business. Our cover was that we were going to hitch the ride and told to keep a low profile.

Lucey had a carry-on case which we squeezed her into, the dog gets too many treats. Anyway, we were ready to resume our journey and when we reached the airport only the pilots knew of the situation.

Agent Smith drove us and dropped us off at the gate, wished us good luck and off she went. Yia, Lucey in the case and I approached our plane. It wasn't a big one, Just about held 100 passengers, the trip was cited for two hours with a contact waiting for us at the other end in San Fran. I felt we were pretty secure and comfortable with the plan. Yia did her share of griping, but I expected some from her. Said she hated flying and why didn't we just take a car, etc, etc. I tuned her out best I could. It was her fault we had to leave the train and still she complained.

As the final passenger boarded it was our turn. I sat in the cockpit with the other two pilots in a jump seat. Introductions were made and they inquired about my charge. I explained she was with the stewardess in the back and was going to keep a low profile for the trip. One could only hope.

The pilots got the go ahead from the tower to lift off and soon the plane was traveling down the runway. As it reach take off speed the front wheels came up and soon were soaring over treetops on the way to the clouds. It was exhilarating.

Next seat belt sign was turned to off and the autopilot click on, the pilot gave the announcement all was well and for the passengers to sit back and enjoy the ride.

Heading over the Rockies came a weather forecast that said we might meet up with some turbulence. Rick, the head pilot said it was uncommon in this area just some up and down bumps. My thoughts turned to Yia who was not happy to fly to begin with, sure hopes she behaves herself.

#35

Yia

A lot of cloak and dagger stuff. Poor Lucy is stuffed in a carry on, Every now and then I get a whimper or a dirty look. Sarge looked real good in that uniform, hope he keeps it, mine is ok… I got some strange looks from the other girls. Seems that stewardesses are a clannish sort; started asking me all kinds of questions.

I tried giving one word answers but this particular girl, Francine was a real pest, I told her I was just hitching a ride and didn't feel like talking. Then the pilot called on their intercom and warned of bumpy weather. Oh No!!! I hate flying. This was a bad idea. Next thing I know, Francine announces that she's pregnant and her morning sickness is kicking in and off to the bathroom she goes. That leaves me and one more woman to look over the passengers; she said that we should go down the aisle and make sure that everyone has their seat belt. Then we hand out pillows and/or blankets to make them comfy, cozy. Who ME?

I told her think we should give them some wine too, actually she said "Good idea, we should." Well, ok!!

I held on to the back of the seats as I made my way up front. There was this young girl, completely terrified at the first bit of turbulence.

I wasn't too happy either. I told her to have a glass of wine to calm her down. Then I said for her to take the whole bottle with a straw. That seemed to make her happy. I actually took a little snort myself. I hate flying.

In row 2 was this older couple were reciting the rosary. I'm all for prayers but they were making the rest of the passengers nervous. I gave them a bottle of wine and two straws and that seemed to quiet them down.

All of a sudden the plane must have dropped 100 feet… everyone started hooting and hollering. Now what?

Hanging on for dear life I managed to get to the front of the group, the girl with the wine bottle had on a big happy grin. Well, she was ok. The other stewardess looked at me and shrugged. Big help she was. Then it came to me, a sing-a–long. That's it. Take their minds off the situation.

I know, I used to entertain at the nursing home and they all loved to sing. I suggested we start with 'Let a Smile Be Your Umbrella' and little by little everyone chimed in. Then we followed with "Pennies from Heaven."

Again another big dip from the plane, it felt like we were riding a runaway elevator. I was running out of tunes then asked for suggestions. The older couple half in the bag by now suggested 'You are my Sunshine,' and we went with that. The plane was rocking and rolling and soon the dips weren't so bad. Actually the nervous girl and the old farts were whopping it up after every dip.

The other Stewardess was busy pouring wine and I think she had a few too. Nobody could be that mellow without help. Francine was still in the bathroom and missing all the fun. Before we knew it we were almost to our destination. I got a big round of applause as everyone staggered off the plane. Actually chant of Yia went up and people asked what plane I was on because they wanted to fly with me again. Am I great of what?

Well, Sarge emerged from the cockpit, shaking his head. I don't know if they were singing in there but he was pretty grumpy. The other two pilots told me I did a great job and missed my calling. If they only know I couldn't wait to get off this contraption.

Francine came out of the bathroom all white and bleary. Said it was the worst time ever for her. She should have come out and joined in.

We all, Sarge the pilots and me waited for everyone to get off the plane. Sarge was very grumpy and I asked him if the plane ride made him sick. " You could say that," was his response.

Our car was waiting for us with another agent behind the wheel. He suggested we change our clothes first chance we got and said the GPS had all the information for us to get to Shirley's.

Of course I wasn't permitted to drive, some regulation or other to keep me from being behind the wheel. The car wasn't bad, actually it was a 4 wheel drive SUV, almost like the Yiamobile but not quite.

We got in, bid the agent adieu and followed the car's direction. Sarge was still quiet with a big scold on his face.

"Is this what I have to look forward to?" I asked?

I got a "Hrrumph" and a sideward glance.

"Ok, Sarge, I don't know what has your shorts in a bunch, but let's clear the air now!"

"You want to clear the air? How could you make a spectacle of yourself on the plane? We are supposed to be traveling incognito and you're up there making a display of yourself. Getting everyone half drunk and being the conductor of your glee club!"

"Whoa, just a minute. What was I suppose to do, the one stewardess, Francine, got sick and didn't come out the bathroom.

The other one and I had a planeload of scared people with all the dips you guys were doing with the plane. I tried calming everyone down including myself. And let me add, you were no help, locked in the cockpit. Can I help it I'm a people person?"

"Yia, what part of witness protection don't you get?" You almost got kidnapped in Chicago, wasn't that a wake up call for you? Some not so nice people are still looking for you and you're making yourself a star? You were supposed to be invisible. How am I to protect you when you are making yourself memorable? Knock it off!"

#36

Lucey

You're not going to believe what they did to me. My buddy, the Sarge and my owner Yia; the two of them stuffed me into this little crate way to small for me then carried me onto a waiting plane. I couldn't do anything except lie down, no room to turn or stretch, nada.

Yia had on some airline costume and the Sarge passed himself of as a pilot. Boy was I doomed, just no justice for us 'four legged protectors of lives and limbs.' I didn't make that up, it was on a dog food commercial.

Yia shoved me under her seat and next thing I know, the big contraption started a slow roll, shivered and shook and lifted off. Meanwhile my crate slides back and nobody notices. What if a door is open, no parachute attached either, I'm calling my ASPCA rep and logging a complaint.

We are in the back where the stewardess's sit and there are refrigerators and a coffee machine. Almost immediately, one of the women, Francine announces she is pregnant and going to be sick. She gets up and runs to the bathroom, never to be seen again. Meanwhile my crate rolls back and forth which each movement of the plane. Yia gets an idea then ties the crate onto the back of her chair. Really, Yia? Just let me out. I can make some friends and get some overdue petting.

Then the plane starts making like a roller coaster, up and down and I'm getting dizzy. Yia and the other lady start making sure everybody is belted in and Yia starts giving out wine. See, no snack for me, write that down, another complaint.

Before you know it, Yia is in front of the plane, leading a sing-a-long. She's in her glory, most of the passengers are in the bag and I'm tied and held hostage in miniature jail. It's a roller coaster, up and down, and up and down. I'm shaking all over with fear. Where's some wine for me?

As soon as I get out of this crate I plan on doing some serious nipping. No more Miss Nice Guy, me!

Oh no…another song from the leader of the group. "My Blue Heaven," I'm cranky and stuffed in here and I'm in need of a treat. Yes, a grilled pork chop at least!

#37

Sarge

I'm trying my best to have patience. It's darn near impossible. How and I suppose to protect someone who makes a spectacle of herself at every chance? How?

The pilots were glad she had the passengers all calmed down. Half plastered more like it. They thought she was great. Am I the only one that realizes the seriousness of the situation? I really should turn her over to another agent. I'm too emotionally involved to be objective. Maybe when we get to Shirley's I'll have a talk with my superior. Ok, I'll try to get control of my feelings and go on with the plan.

From the San Francisco airport to our destination is about 10 hours by car. That means an overnight stay someplace. I asked Yia to check out the hotels/motels along our route and call and make a reservation for tonight. I could go with a stiff drink and a good steak. A place with a good restaurant is a must.

I was waiting for the usual pleas from Yia asking to drive, but so far nothing. Maybe she got the message from last trip. Actually, I would let her drive but there isn't enough booze to calm me down when she's behind the wheel. I don't know how Lucey goes with her.

I called ahead and told George of our change in plans, he was most accommodating. Said Shirley was anxious to see us both and he could use some guy talk. It must get boring in the winter with extra time on your hands. I wonder if George still likes to cook. I could use a real homemade food. Anyway I looked over and saw Yia nodding. Probably coming down from all that adrenaline she had, I know how much she hates to fly. I must admit she was a trooper but to get the whole plane rocking? I'll try to have more patience with her, it can't be easy separated from her big family. I'll also check in with my boss to see what's happening with the motorcycle guys. The trouble at the train station was unnerving. Jose and his friends sure helped, I'll drop him a line to when I get to Shirley and George's.

Well, the monotony of the road has lulled Yia to sleep so I have peace for a while. The highway moved swiftly and I need to take a rest, get some coffee and use the john. I was looking for a service center and drove about another 30 miles before one came into view. I slowed down and parked. Yia was still asleep and I was reluctant to wake her. I sat in the car for a while hoping the cessation of movement would rouse her. But no, she was out like a light. I carefully took out the ignition keys and then got out and locked the doors. I was hoping to get back before she woke up and wondered where I was. I took Lucey with me to the dog station and put her back in the car. Yia was still out like a light. Okay, I'll make it quick and bring her back a snack.

I couldn't believe the long lines for everything. The bathroom, the coffee bar and the snack station all had people cued up. This was going to take longer than I thought. I was getting nervous and after using the men's room I hurried back to the car.

Getting back to the vehicle, I realized that the front right tire was flat as a pancake and Yia and Lucey were missing. Gone!! This can't be happening! Who? How? I thought we were safe! I was pulling out my cell phone only to remember I left it in the car.

OH No!! I started feeling the blood creep up my neck and a cold sweat broke out. She couldn't have been kidnapped because of my failure to protect her. I was sitting on the curb trying to think of what to do. What to do?

As I thought of some options a dog ran up and started licking my faced, then a pair of big feet wearing sneakers appeared. Attached to them were the legs of my ward. I couldn't believe it, I was so relieved I started yelling at Yia.

Before any words came out, she asked what I was doing? She was looking all over for me. I then realized I was sitting by the wrong car. Same make and model but wrong car. I'm an idiot!!

I grabbed Yia and gave her a giant bear hug. I was never so happy to see anyone, even that dog. I then knew how much she meant to me and vowed to be more patient with her. Granted, she's a handful, but life around her is never dull.

"Com'on Yia, let me buy you some coffee and I may even let you drive for a while."

"You sure Sarge? You're not sick or anything? Okay, give me the keys before you change your mind."

"No Yia, I'm just tired. Let's get moving before I get a second wind and change my mind."

With that she pulled me up and we headed to the rest stop to load up on snack and coffee. I even got Lucey a treat. The next two days of driving should go easily. I'll never do that again. Where I go she'll go, my heart can't take the strain again.

#38

Yia

I'm starting to worry about Sarge. The stress is getting to him and he's making mistakes. Good thing I am still sharp as a tack. After we got some refreshments and left deposits in the bathrooms, we headed back to the right car. Geez Louise, he even let me drive without a big fuss and all the noise he made before. Maybe I should take his temperature; he isn't acting like the Sarge of old.

Anyway, it wasn't long into the drive before he nodded off. I traveled along Route 80 onto Route 805 for a short distance. Next I got on Route 5 that was to take us up to Salem Oregon. Shirley and George have their vineyard on the outskirts. I am getting so anxious to see them both.

Sarge was still sleeping when I pulled into Shasta Lake. They had a nice hotel with a good restaurant there; a nice place for us to unwind and rest. I woke him and got out and stretched my weary bones, Lucey was making friends with all the valets and anyone that would give her attention. Really! When is she going to slow down?

We checked in, got adjoining rooms; then went to refresh ourselves before dinner. I couldn't believe how beautiful California is, lots of mountains and big trees. The folks here are so nice, I can see the appeal of the West Coast.

As I was getting myself all gussied up, Sarge knocked on the door and invited me for a drink before dinner. Wow, this is like a date or something. "Sure, be out in a sec." Then I put on an extra layer of lip stick. Yeah, I was looking good.

We met in the hall and went downstairs to the cocktail lounge. I felt like a young girl again, better not pass any mirrors. A glass of wine for me and Sarge had himself a scotch on the rocks. On to the dining room that was not too crowded and we ate leisurely and talked about the events of the day, leaving out the part where Sarge forgot where he parked.

There was a piano player and although I wanted to sing, Sarge shot me down before I made a move. Reminded me to keep a low profile. Just when can I be me again? It's so hard to waste all this talent. He's being so nice, I caved. This time at least.

Dinner over, we went up to our rooms, I realized what a long day it had been and started to feel weary. In the morning a few more hours of driving and then we'll see Shirley and George. I can hardly wait. Hopefully the Sarge will get some information about the so called baddies that want retribution from me. How rude! It wasn't like I narced on any of them. Could I help it if Lucey was the squealer without me knowing it? It's always the innocent that suffer. Moi!!

Sarge walked me to my room and before we said "Good Night" he leaned over and gave me a peck on my cheek. It was totally unexpected but somehow I felt euphoric. It's been a while since I had any male attention and I forgot how alluring I can be. Ah yes, I walzed into the room on air and lay down on the bed just reliving my good night peck. Maybe soon I'll discover what's in that box.

#39

Lucey

There's something fishy going on. I'm not sure yet what it is, but something isn't kosher. Yia, who is always complaining about Sarge and gets into a tizzy every time she thinks about the box, has mellowed out.

How do I know, well I'll give you the skinny. Seems that Sarge picked her up and they went out to dinner. Then he walks her back to her door and I guess they were both loaded, he gives her a goodnight peck on the cheek. How do I know? Well, in she comes like a teenager, swooning. Yeah, swooning; holding on to the kissed cheek and prancing around in her support hose in a trance.

She never even notices me, sits herself down on the bed, still holding the just kissed cheek and falls backwards into a stupor.

Hey, I need a walk, if you haven't noticed Yia, it's past 11PM. I'm overdue. I have no choice but to interrupt her moment, it's either that or whiz on the floor, which will get me yelled at. Either way I'm going to be in deep dodo whichever way I play this. At least on the train I had some walkers.

I decide to let her be and go and scratch on the adjoining room door. You know the one that has the Sarge in it. By now I'm walking cross legged, no easy feat for someone with four legs. He opens the door looking past me. I had to nip his ankle to get his attention. Then he hops around yelping and screaming. Who was expecting at the door? Don't answer that. I will gouge my eyes out.

Finally, he spots me and sees the predicament I'm in, looks past Yia still in La La land and decides to take me out.

Whew, I hardly made it to that small patch of grass in the courtyard. Now how about a pork chop?

Guess that was out. I am brought back upstairs and thrown into Yia's room and the door shut quietly.

Yia finally breaks out of her daze and says, "Oh my goodness Lucey, you need a walk!"

Guess what? Yep, I get a second walk of the night. Yia is wondering why I took the opportunity to sniff al the bushes and trees just for good measure and I was not in big hurry.

Not to keep her wondering, I faked a couple of whizzes and then she was happy. Still got it, hope she never catches on.

#40
Yia

Almost time to leave this hotel. It's been very refreshing, I feel 20 years younger. Lucey slept most of the night, right after her walk she settled down and both of us went off to dream land. I am so excited about today, at the finish of this trip we will see Shirley and her husband George. I can't wait. I have a few things to give them but hugs from Yia.

Yia's will be best of all.

Sarge is knocking on our adjoining door. We had a swell evening last night. Almost perfect if I didn't have to interrupt my reverie to walk Lucey; can't have it all I guess.

Time to leave, going for a little exercise for Lucey and me then on to the last leg of this journey. We discussed the driving while at breakfast and agreed we would share it. Amazing, right? I'll try my best not to show off or complain about how slow he goes. Sometimes he drives like an old man.

Sarge took the first lap of the road trip and I sat back and thought about my friend Shirley. She sure was interesting. Lucey loves her to pieces and she has a special rapport with her. That and they both love milk bones that they eat together. I remember some of Shirley obsessions with her chicken psychoses, yeah, the good old days.

Looking back I found her sitting on the eggs on Shop-Rite. Then there was her sitting in the hay in the chicken coop on that cranky farmers place. She was so content. Yeah, what's the harm in being a chicken?

I recall when she first met George, that didn't go so well. Seems he asked her to come to dinner that he was making. Said the main course was kota. He never explained that kota in Greek was chicken. No, it was when he served it, Shirl freaked out, called George no lover of poultry, grabbed the roast chicken ran off and proceeded to give the chicken a burial at sea. She tossed it off a bridge into the river.

That left George very confused and amazing enough he cared for Shirley to help her get better then asked her to marry him. What a fairy tale, I am so happy for her. They live on a small vineyard in Oregon and specialize in some kind of fancy white wine. George said the soil in Oregon is similar to the soil in his homeland island of Chios, Greece.

Now that winter is settling in, grapes are picked and now their fruit are in vats fermenting or whatever it does to become wine.

I'm sure I will be able to sample the finished products. You just never know where life will lead you.

I looked over at Sarge driving and thought about our previous evening. The word magical came to mind, hard to associate that with Sarge, but I guess there are things about him that I don't know. He's not a bad sort in fact his overprotective attitude towards me is very endearing. Makes me wonder again about what is in that mysterious box.

Sometimes I think I should settle down and have somebody in my life again. Someone I can share the day with, someone who lived in my generation and knows the history. Now that he has his farting under control he could fill the bill.

Well, I hope that this little vaykay relaxes us both and I can catch up with my friend. Almost time for me to get behind the wheel and drive. I sure do like to zip around. The roads here are a little curvy and the speed limit changes with the terrain. That's okay, I never pay attention to them anyway.

#41

Sarge

The scenery around here is amazing. So clean and refreshing the further north we go. Yia has been especially quiet today. I know she's just itching to drive. Such a competitive spirit; she likes living on the fringe. Not at all like my dear departed wife. No, she was calm and quiet Unlike Yia who has a million things going on at one time. We never had any children, but Yia has kids coming out of the woodwork. She even has some that call her Mom that she adopted along the way; then the grandkids, the original Dirty Dozen and a whole bunch of spares.

When I think about the future I'm not sure I am ready for such a peripatetic life style. She's a nice lady, but exhausting, time will tell. Now I am looking forward to seeing George and his vineyard. Time to pull over and switch drivers. Maybe I'll nod off so I don't flinch at every turn, it's hard knowing how Yia whips her car around. This one is a bit of a slug so she can't get too crazy.

Giving up the wheel, I must have been tired so before long I found myself nodding. Traffic was nonexistence, just an occasional car or pick up truck on the opposite lane. The ennui lolled me to sleep and suddenly I was jerked awake with brakes screeching. My harness restraint prevented me from hitting the dashboard and then I fell back hard on the seat. Waking up I heard the sounds of police sirens coming.

"What did you do now Yia," I yelled? I couldn't help myself, the woman is always in the middle of some kind of crisis. She stared at me for a second and then I wanted to know how she could get into a jam on such a quiet road. The louder I yell, the more quiet she became, then the police car with sirens blaring passed us by at warp speed. Oops! Yia turned to me staring and told me to get out of the car.

"What? You can't leave me stranded on a highway with no place to go? What's your problem? Just because I got startled you are ready to throw me out into the unknown?" I was stupefied.

"You have your phone and badge, call a cop or a cab, but if you stay in the car we will say some nasty things to each other and I prefer to be alone," was her answer.

"Listen, Yia, I was startled. I'm sorry if I thought the cops were after you. You are usually in the middle of one calamity or other. That's the reason we are on this trip to begin with. Be reasonable."

Yia replied with one word, "Out!"

"Fine, you're on your own. Good Luck!" and with that I got out and slammed the door. She exhausts me, always on the brink of one disaster or another. I walked over to a clump of trees and sat down on a fallen log to think about what to do next, watching her pull out onto the road. I think I aged 20 years since I have been on this assignment. I looked around; I was in the middle of Nowheresville. I took a minute to compose myself as Yia pulled away. I was really steamed at her and need to reduce my surging blood pressure.

I felt ridiculous calling the police, what do I say, "My protectee threw me out of the car?" That would raise some eyebrows and get me in hot water. No, I better think on this some more.

As I sat on the log trying to decide my next move, a friendly farmer pulled up and asked if I need a ride. "That would be great. I was headed to the OPA Vineyard, do you know where that is?" "Sure, do. Sonny, you're just about 100 feet from the driveway on the right. Do you want a lift, it's not far."

"No thanks," I replied and started walking down the shoulder of the road. Sure enough around the bend in the road was a big sign mounted on the entrance to the OPA Vineyards.

Yia must have known how close it was, and then as I started down the entrance road, I saw the car was parked and Yia was taking Lucey for a walk.

She saw me coming and asked if I was myself yet? Sheepishly, I said I was and I was sorry that I yelled at her. She just told me to drive and that she needed a little time herself to calm down. Lucey greeted me like I was gone for days, but that's Luce.

The long driveway opened up to a large house with some outbuildings behind. Racing down the road were Shirley and George. We got out and greeted them. Lucey was all over Shirley and Yia and Shirl had a big silly grins on their faces. I shook hands with George and watched the welcoming party.

I sure hope Yia can forgive my outburst, it wasn't like she hasn't caused all sorts of commotions in the past. She seemed happy enough as I followed her and Shirley into the house with George.

It was good to finally get here and get some down time. Maybe I can speak to George about what an idiot I was; he probably had a few experiences himself.

#42

Lucey

I saw Shirley and George walking towards the car. I went completely crazy trying to get out and greet my bestest friend, Shirley. Finally Sarge stopped the car and Yia and he ran out leaving me behind. I scratched furiously on the window and Yia turned around and opened my door.

I ran as fast of my stumpy legs could manage and Shirley bent down and swooped me up. I licked her face and she licked mine and it was nirvana. She whipped out some milk bones and we both ate one together. I'm glad she still likes them, I was worried about having treats.

George and Sarge were shaking hands and Yia and Shirl were both talking and crying at the same time. No sniffing each other, I guess humans don't do that yet. It's an evolution thing.

Boy, it was so great to see Shirley; I didn't realize how much I missed her. It looks to me that George's cooking added a few pounds to Shirley's usually thin self. Now she is not exactly a tubby but full figured like me. I kept running around her in circles and then laying down for her to scratch my tummy. Oh, what joy!!! Yia kept interrupting our meeting by talking to Shirl. I wish Yia would pay attention to Sarge or somebody so I can have some alone time with my best buddy. How rude!!

George was giving Sarge a tour of the vineyard and telling him all kinds of boring stuff. I was just content to get some over due belly rubs from Shirl. Boy oh boy it was so good to see her.

While the guys wandered off together, Shirley took Yia and me into their home, a nice old fashion farmhouse with a huge kitchen for George's love of cooking. Yia and Shirl talked at once to each other, it was hard to get a bark in edgewise. Guess I'll have to wait until they come up for air.

Meanwhile I spied a big old dog asleep in the corner of the room. I over heard Shirley telling Yia that he came with the house and his name was Smoky. He probably liked cigars or something. He wasn't very interested in being friends, barely raised his head, so I left him alone, for now. I'll bother him later once I look around.

#43

George

Finally Sarge and Yia Yia arrived. Shirley has been waiting anxiously for their arrival and had herself in a tizzy with worry. Ever since Yia left the train all I heard was Shirley lamenting about how much Yia hated to travel by plane. My little Kukla* is running so fast to greet them I'm afraid she may fall, still has her streak of dare devil in her.

We met up with them and that dog Lucey; Shirley, Yia and Lucey were all prancing around talking at one time. I figure I'd go and greet the Sarge. He looked a little dishevel and it's probably the long journey taking its toll. I need to ask him if he was positive that no baddies knew where they were. No sense in exposing Kukla and me to danger if possible. He assured me that all was well and that's why they left the train. The last leg of this trip they did by car with no sign of being followed. That was good enough for me.

Next I told Sarge a little bit about of our lives here on this vineyard; actually when he asked if I bought it, I had to tell him I had it on lease with an option. Meanwhile, I'm seeing how we adjust to the quiet life it affords. Keeping Shirley happy was my biggest priority, she would like a bit more activity, and so time will tell.

As we walked around, Sarge asked me where the grapes were; I told him that I sold them. There's a fellow that owns the neighboring vineyard that buys grapes. He then makes wine and has all the equipment that bottles it and has a tasting room. That's my hesitation, the outlay it will take for me to start making my own wine. I would need a press, destemmer, holding tanks in addition to the bottling. Also I would need to build a tasting room and hire some part timers to run it. It's a giant outlay for the startup and I'm not sure this is where Shirley wants to live, she more of a people person, plus I am worried about her.

Sarge was quiet at first: absorbing all the information I just gave him. He asked me exactly what had me concerned. I told needed him to keep this information in confidence, that I didn't want Yia Yia to know, but I really needed to tell someone who could understand. That would be Sarge, I'm so glad I can finally share this with someone I can trust.

He's an officer of the law and I realized he thought I might be telling him of a broken law or something like that. I assured him it was nothing illegal, just a worry that probably didn't mean much, but it does have me concerned. I guess the suspense made him impatient and I got a raised eyebrow and a quizzical look.

Well, I said this much, I had to level with him. " It's about Shirley, Sarge, she has me worried."

"How so? She seems happy now," he said.

"I am pretty sure she's happy and in a good place but there's a couple of things that makes me worry. You know I'm Greek, natural born worriers."

He kept the staring and hunched his shoulders, I guess being I leveled with him so far it would be a relief to finally tell someone. "Sarge, I think she clucks!"

"What?"

"Clucks"

Sarge digested that for a while and asked if she clucks all day? "No, no Sarge, she only clucks when she sleeps," I told him. "I'm not sure she even remembers it during the day, she seems so normal, but at night when she asleep the clucking begins."

Sarge kicked the dirt around his feet and scratched his head. I'm sure he was puzzled about this information. I've been nervous ever since it began, about 3 months ago. Every night when Shirley is sound asleep she begins clucking, once she reached over to me and felt around the bed. I think she was looking for eggs. I wasn't ready to share this information with him just yet. What I did need was an idea on what to do next before she wakes up and start looking for a better looking rooster.

*Koukla, Greek Doll

#44

Shirley

OMG!! They're really here!!! My best friends in the whole world; I can't believe how much I missed them. Yia looks great and Lucey, just as cute and frisky as ever. Lucey and I romped around the yard for a while, greeting each other. What a sight for sore eyes.

And my dear friend Yia, she doesn't look a day over 70. She kept telling Lucey to "knock it off!" but Lucey and I paid no heed. It's been a long time between dog hugs and licks. Finally we calmed down and I could get some much-needed Yia Yia hugs. Boy, I'm so glad they are here.

We walked around the grounds for a while and then I took them to our horse barn. There were a few horses we have and my favorite was a big black stallion called Mercury. I think Lucey was a bit put off by the huge size of him. She stayed behind Yia as we went from stall to stall. I told Yia that I ride every morning and she should come with me. She said maybe but said also that she hadn't ridden in a long time and needed a slow horse. I remember her time with Slug and how she gave him some pep pills to liven him up. That didn't work out so well but it's how she met Sarge. So some good came out of it, I think.

I asked her what's going on and she was a bit reluctant to tell me. Seems they have been getting under each other's skin lately and she's annoyed with him right now. I'll wait for a different time.

Next she remarked that I put on a little weight since she saw me last. I'll say, I gained close to 40 pounds. All of George's great cooking and my secret habit. I guess I need some help and maybe she can steer me in the right direction. I'll always be grateful for her support when I was obsessed with chickens.

"Yia, there's something I have to tell you in confidence. I need help." I was a little embarrassed but she my best friend in the whole world, who else can I turn to?

Her first question was whether or not I was back in chicken mode.

"No, positively not, Yia! This is a little different but I can't help myself, I crave and crave and crave. Even at night I think about it while I'm asleep." I told her.

"Are you sure Shirley, I don't want you sitting on eggs in the Shop-Rite dairy section again. What is the current problem and how can I help?"

Isn't she great? I am so happy I can finally tell someone my dark secret and get some advice. Bless Yia, she always knows what to do.

I was a little embarrassed but I felt a weight being lifted off my shoulders as I explained to her my dilemma.

"Well, Yia here it is, I think I have to go back into re-hab. I can't seem to help myself." "Rehab? For what?" was her question.

"I need to go somewhere where I kick my addition to choco-late. A chocolate rehab." I was totally ashamed to admit to an-other addition but I can't live like this any more. "Please help me

Yia. I don't know where to turn. "I wouldn't stop the tears from flowing, it was painful, and I couldn't live anymore without my chocolate. Any kind, from semisweet chocolate morsels, to peanut butter cups, a stash of Hersey bars in the barn, some under the bed, chocolate wrappers everywhere. I don't want George to know. He's been through enough with me. I admit it, I am a chocolate junkie."

Yia just sat and listened, she was wide eyed and I can tell she was trying to think. I realized that it was a lot to ask, but she was all I had, the only one I trusted to give me the best advice.

"Shirley, I don't know if there is a chocolate rehab facility. If there are, I am sure we would have known. Have you tried cold turkey? You know that sometimes people swap one addition for another. Actually, chocolate addition isn't so bad."

"Oh Yia, I tried cold turkey but I was weak, I made it through two days and then the sweats and the chills came followed by the shakes. It was awful; I even tried to steal a kid's tootsie roll from him. I'm resorting to crime to feed my habit."

"Even while I am asleep I dream of chocolate, how I am trying to get the peanut butter off the roof of my mouth, one night I dreamt I spill my M&M's all over the bed and was searching for them when I woke up George. Actually, I startled him and I pretended to be asleep. It's getting out of control. What am I going to do?"

"I admit Shirl that I don't know too much about chocolate addition, however, with any addition you have to admit the problem and seek help. That's what you are doing now. Next you have to confess the situation to George, I'm sure he loves you and would help. Listen, it's not the worst thing in the world, we can do it together . Okay?"

Wow, I felt better already, I will kick this habit and move on with my life. I knew Yia was the answer. I'll probably give my stash to her.

#45

Lucey

United at last. Just like Thelma and Louise, Starsky and Hutch, Martin and Lewis…on and on. It was great seeing them together, Shirley is my bestest human friend and Yia, she's ah ……. Yia. They had their heads together as we walked the vineyard. Something sure was troubling Shirley, I could tell she had a problem on her mind.

We went into the horse stable, yikes, it stunk in there and those horses were huge. Some cats ran around and Shirley had a pet Jack Russell Terrier Rocky, who thought he owned the place. I'll see about that later. Shirley showed Yia the horse she rides. This enormous black stallion named Mercury and pointed out a smaller stable mate that she thought would suit Yia. No mention of me. How rude!!

I overheard Shirley telling Yia about her love of chocolate. Dogs can't have any because it's supposed to toxic to wee creatures. What a way to go… I had vision of having a bath in the stuff. Why is everything I like bad for me? Bones, chocolate, grapes, bad boy dogs the list goes on.

There's no justice, no justice at all.

Enough about me, Yia had Shirley convinced to do an intervention to admitting her problem to those she loved and know we would support her recovery. At least that's the stuff she was telling Shirley.

Shirley looked less than convinced. On one side she wanted to break her habit, on the other she was hooked and didn't want to quit. I can relate, it took all my will power to break it off with Roscoe, my dream dog. My destiny, I yearn for him still, oh the pain!!

After wallowing in some well-deserved self-pity, I gathered myself up and went in search of that snooty Jack Russell. I was sure he was giving me the once over in the barn. You can't tell me he doesn't miss me and all my charms. Can I help it is I am just a magnet and possessed of an alluring personality?

Yia tries to contain my charisma but there's just so much she can do. No sense in wasting it, I'm not getting any younger. FYI neither is she. I think it's a rapidly aging syndrome that she has developed and I'm keeping my distance, just in case it's catching.

#46
Yia

Walking and talking with Shirley has me concerned. She admitted to me that she is powerless on her desire for chocolate. She's embarrassed to tell George, afraid of losing his respect and love. I tried my best to convince her that she needed his support to break her habit. I don't know, I don't think she's ready to stop her addition.

Actually, she told me that George is the one that got her hooked. Always making some beautiful concoction with plenty of chocolate icing and filling. Just talking about it she got all dreamy and took off in search of a fix.

First a chicken and now this, I needed to confide in Sarge but right know he not one of my favorite people. He totally over reacted to the sirens, thinking I caused the patrol car to be after me. I admit that I sometimes was in the middle of a situation or two, but the man has a poor opinion of me and that is bothersome. Hrrmph!

I strolled around for a while and met Shirley coming out of the barn. Seems she has a stash hidden in a variety of places. We walked quietly and then she asked if I thought she could be cured. "Sure Shirl, it was a lot harder to stop being a chicken, this should be easy."

"You're right Yia, the longer I wait the harder it will be. I think I'm ready for the intervention. I just hope I don't lose George over this. He is trying so hard to keep me happy. I never met anyone so selfless."

Just be gentle with him. Okay?"

So I guess my next step is to tell Sarge and for us to plan to get Shirley some help. I don't know if there is a chocolate hotline or a Chocolate Anonymous. If there isn't there should be. Hey, maybe I'm on to something. Yes, Shirley needs a project and she's a real good people person. I bet she would be a great consular to those in need of breaking their habit. Just think of all the chocolate lovers out there that are powerless to stop. I don't know where I get these great genius ideas. Must be my fate in life.

Now I had to plan an intervention, had to get Shirley some help. I didn't think it was so bad, but what if accelerates? She might get into a life of crime. Stealing chocolate bars or worse, robbing a candy store. I could just image the pressure at Easter time with all those chocolate bunnies around. No, it's time for action.

Well, first things first, Sarge and I will settle in and I'll tell him of the situation. He has helped before and he might have some ideas on how to support her. Besides, George will need a man's shoulder to cry on. He's Greek you know, very emotional people.

Shirley and I walked around the vineyard for a while. It was great just being here with her. I didn't realize how much I missed her. We walked and talked and remember the days we thought we were Thelma and Louise; the good old days.

I looked around but I didn't see Lucey. "Shirley, didn't Lucey follow you into the barn?" I asked.

"Come to think of it Yia, she did, why isn't she here? Oh my, Rocky and she were following me and he knows where I keep my stash of candy. You don't think?"

And with that both Shirley and I raced back to the barn, there was Lucey and the Jack Russell Terrier, Rocky were in some sort of coma. They were on their back semi-conscience. All around them were candy wrappers torn open. They must have eaten their fill and passed out.

"Shirley, how much candy do you think they ate? What was it?

I think we have to get them to a Vet and quickly!"

"Oh no Yia, Rocky's George's dog. If something happens to him, George will be devastated. This is my entire fault, come. Let's take my car."

I picked up Lucey, whose tongue was hanging out of the side of her mouth, traces of chocolate still on it. Shirley took Rocky and then me Rocky and Lucey got into the back seat. I needed to get some paper towels in case they start to get sick. I got out and ran back into the barn where I saw ripped open bags of semi-sweet morsels, lots of Hersey bars wrappers and assorted bags of M&M's all strewn around. Those dogs consumed a lot of chocolate. This is Shirley's fault. She is truly a chocoholic!!

Racing back to the car, with paper towels and some baby wipes, I got in and Shirley sped down the driveway to the Vet's office. I prayed hard that we weren't too late.

Shirley parked and helped me get out the car with the dogs, we ran to the Vet's office and were met by his assistants. Thank God for car phones. Pacing back in forth in the waiting room, Shirley vowed never to eat chocolate again. I called Sarge and told him the situation and he said he would tell George and meet us in a little while.

What seemed like a lifetime, the Vet came out and said the dogs were going to be all right. He had pumped their stomachs and remarked on how much chocolate was in each dog. Said our quick action probably saved their lives. They had to stay over night but he felt we could pick them up in the AM.

I looked at Shirley and she had tears streaming down her face, It must have been a great relief for her. I knew Lucey would be OK, nothing but a silver bullet is going to get her.

Sarge and George ran through the door and we gave them the good news. George was asking how did this happen and that's when Shirley confessed to eating copious amounts of chocolate, that she was addicted to it, in fact she said she was a chocoholic. Without saying a word, George just turned and went outside, leaving Shirley dumb founded.

#47

Sarge

I made sure the girls were all right and then I left in search of George. I found him sitting in the car with his bowed head in his hands. At first I thought of giving him a moment but there was no time like the present. I went over to the other side of the car and got in. I could see the distress in his face, I assured him that Rocky was going to be fine, that dogs get into the craziest stuff but he interrupted me.

"No Sarge, I know Rocky will be fine, no I am upset about Shirley," was his reply. "But why George? Is it the chicken thing again?" I asked as gently as I could. "No Sarge, it's not that, she confided in Yia Yia that she is a chocoholic, a chocoholic? All this time I thought she was reverting back to her chicken persona and it was not that! Why couldn't she tell me? I am her husband and my Kukla Moo* wouldn't tell me? Where have I failed her?"

Oh boy! I thought for a while and said I thought that she was afraid that he might leave her, that she was ashamed. I really didn't know that much about their relationship but I understood how much hurt he must be in with Shirley not trusting him. It was easy to see the pain he was in. I told him that Shirley was planning an intervention where she was seeking help from her close friends and him. That she was working up her courage when this problem with the dogs occurred.

"Yes, my friend, I understand, but it still hurts she needed other people and not able to confide in me. No, she had to have her addition hidden from me, why?" I couldn't answer him on that but I said that we should go home and try to get back on course, if that's what he wanted.

"Yes, let's do that. Yia can take Shirley and you and I will go home, feed the animals and plan, okay?" "Sure George," I answered, "let's get back to normal, whatever that is."

All the way home George stayed quiet. He was thinking and worrying and I was at a loss to help him. I just hope we can get George and Shirley back on track. Goodness knows if she leaves him, Shirl'll be back at Yia's and then more wild shenigans from the two of them. This can't happen once is enough to watch, isn't this supposed to be a time for slowing down?

*Koukla Moo, Greek for my doll

#48

George

I sat with the Sarge, I know he was trying to comfort me. We were heading to the vineyard; it's time to feed the animals. I just think he doesn't understand. He's a widower and had a long time marriage, but marriage is different things to different people.

Trying to explain myself to him was difficult. Shirley and I got married in the Greek Church tradition. We shared our crowns tied together by ribbons that signified that we were the King and the Queen of our household. We sipped the holy wine from the same challis, we held the candle, we circled the altar three times our first journey into our married life. We were no longer a half, now we were whole; two people sharing one life. We respect each other as we respect ourselves.

I took a long time before I married. I was looking for the one woman who would share the same vision of marriage that I had. I thought Shirley was the one.

How can I explain the to Sarge? I feel betrayed that Shirley couldn't come to me for something so trivial. Chocoholic, big deal! I would give her a bath in chocolate if she wanted. No, she waited until Yia came before she could reveal what troubled her. My marriage is a sham, she doesn't respect it enough to turn to me in time of strife.

I could feel my sorrow passing and the void filling with anger.

We arrived home and I busied myself with work. I think I should calm down before Shirley gets here. There's no need to air this problem in front of our guests. No I'll carry on and wait for another time.

I am also wondering if this vineyard is too quiet for Shirley's temperament. She's so used to more excitement, seems I'm not enough. I can work anywhere; I'll try and speak to her tonight in the privacy of our bedroom. Maybe we should go back East to a more populated place.

My mind is racing, I am thinking of several things at once. Time to take Mercury out for a ride. It will help to get my thoughts together.

By the time I got back dinner was on the table. There was a certain hush to the room. Everyone missed the dogs, me included. Conversation was light and I said it was a long day. I for one was going to retire early and get and jump on tomorrow's chores so we could pick up the dogs early.

Shirley was especially quiet that evening, I think she was guilty about the stash of her chocolates that the dogs got into. Well, she has to deal with that. Actions have consequences and she picked poorly. I wasn't ready to give her more pain so I rolled over and went to sleep. Needless to say, I slept fitfully all night, wondering what road to chose. I think I will seek the advice of our Priest. He may have a better insight than me, no he'll see things without the cloud of pain.

The next morning, I got up early I fed the horses and then drove my car to the little Greek Church in town. I attended mass and waited until it was over and the people left to approach our pastor, Father Socrates Pappadopoulous. He could tell I was troubled and directed me to his study. "So George, what is on your mind? I haven't seen you or your lovely wife in a while. It must be serious for you to be here so early."

He sat back in his chair scratching his graying beard as I related the events of yesterday and how betrayed I felt that my wife had more confidence in her friend then in me. She didn't trust or respect me enough to confide her problems with me and I was upset.

"Well George," he said, "I can understand that your feelings are real and that you are hurt. That's the problem of counseling; you may not like some suggestions. As I see it, you think you have the right to be jealous of her friend but instead of being glad she is seeking help you are mad that it was her friend and not you that Shirley chose. Right so far?"

"Yes Father, that's it, she didn't have enough faith or respect in our marriage to tell me of her pain," I marveled at his insight. "So instead of being supportive, you made it all about you. You need to forgive her and yourself for being jealous of her longtime friend. I think Shirley looks upon her as a mother figure. You wouldn't be so jealous of Shirley's mother would you?"

"I don't know Father, I think I would be hurt she didn't tell me her problem, I thought that's what being married was, respect and trust."

"Ah George, it is also about forgiveness, forgive yourself first and then talk to Shirley and support her in her time of need." He told me. "Actually, you never told me, what is this terrible problem?"

"Oh Father, Shirley thinks she is a chocoholic, do you know of any programs for that?"

"This is your terrible problem? You should be glad it is something so trivial. You should hear the people's problems that come to me. Get a grip and be a man. You come here and waste my time with a woman eating too much chocolate? Really? Go home and be happy, you haven't passed the marriage test my son. Your wife didn't share her situation with you. I can understand why now. You are insecure. There is help for that but no place that I know of treats people eating too much chocolate. Maybe Weight Watchers!"

Well that was sobering; I sought out help and got a lecture. Maybe he is right. I am making it about me, I should be happy that this is the least of my troubles. I have to be more open with Shirley; my worries are small compared to others. I needed that kick in the butt. What a smart man our priest is, He made me feel better already. I think I'll run past the Vet's office to see if the dogs are ready to go.

Life is complicated but I made my troubles out of something minor. I know we Greeks are emotional people but I needed that reality check.

I stopped and got the dogs, they didn't look any the worse for their misadventure into chocolate cuisine. I will talk to Shirley then we will decide together our next step. I can't imagine my life without her.

#49

Shirley

I guess I made a mess of everything. My dear friends are here and already there is a crisis with me in the middle of it all. I know George is upset with me. I'm upset with me. I didn't realize how much my problem could affect everyone. It started small, one chocolate bar at a time and then it became an addition. I began to crave chocolate all the time. I know I was putting on extra weight but I didn't care. It became too much of a good thing. I started hiding my chocolate everywhere. In fact right now I can't wait for a few minutes alone to check on my other stash I hope the dogs didn't fine. I swear I will only eat a little. I'll wean myself a little each day until I have it under control.

Oh, who am I kidding? I know I have to go cold turkey, I don't want to, but. I know I can lean on Yia Yia, but I can't hurt George anymore than I have. Maybe they should have the intervention and I can draw strength from everybody. Meanwhile I'll just check and make sure the dogs don't eat anymore chocolate. It seems like it's toxic for all of us.

It's all so complicated, here I thought getting married and living on this beautiful vineyard would be my dream come true. It is turning into a nightmare and I am the cause.

Let me see, oh yes! It's still here! Oh that sweet smell, the call of the sugar and cocoa… I have to eat only one, just to take the edge off.

"Shirley are you in here?"

Yikes, it's Yia. I don't care. I'll give her a Milky Way and she'll go away.

"Shirley what are you doing? There are candy wrappers all around you and you have chocolate dribbling out of your mouth! You're out of control! Quick come with me and get to the house, George will be back any minute now and he can't see you like this.!"

"Yia, leave me alone! I need this! I want this! You can't possibly understand!"

"Shirley, I understand you feel powerless to control your urges, but is it worth all you work for? Your marriage? Your self-respect? Put down that Hersey Bar and get up and come with me."

I got up to go and that's the last thing I remembered.

#50
Yia

I was walking out of the barn with Shirley, talking a mile a minute when I realized she wasn't there. I turned around thinking she went to get more chocolate when I saw her laying on the ground. "Get up Shirl, what are you doing?" She was unresponsive. I rushed over and checked her out. Her pulse was fast and her face was all flushed, I screamed for help and Sarge and George came running out of the house.

"Quick one of you dial 911, tell them there is an unconscious woman needing help." Sarge called and came over. "What do you think it is Yia? The ambulance and paramedics are on their way. Is there any thing we came do meanwhile?"

"Let's turn her on her side Sarge, in case she vomits and try to find a blanket to cover her." George came over and knelt down beside her, he was visibly shaken and distraught. "Don't worry George, she'll be okay in a few hours. I think I know now why she has this addiction to sweets."

He didn't say much just sat there brushing Shirley's hair from her face and holding her hand for dear life. I started to worry about him. In the distance I could hear the ambulance's siren. Good, they should be here soon.

Sarge went up to the driveway and waited for their arrival, he then directed them to the stable area. A big white truck with a driver and paramedic stopped and one jumped out. The paramedic, a young man in his early 20's examined Shirley and questioned me. He and his partner put her on the stretcher and started and IV and did an EKG. Reports were radioed into the hospital emergency room and interpreted with directions sent back.

I was glad to see that they hooked her up to normal saline. She didn't need any more sugar. In fact I thought she was in a diabetic coma.

Sort of explains her overwhelming craving for sweets. I started to remember that she was always thirsty and running to the bathroom a lot. With Shirley who can say what is normal?

As soon as she was in the ambulance the paramedic got in and took her to the nearest hospital. Sarge, George and I followed behind. I kept reassuring George that she would be OK, then I told him what I thought. That Shirley is a diabetic and that caused her to seek out the worst possible thing, sugar. Diabetics crave it, but it can be treated. George was so preoccupied with nerves that I doubt he heard a word.

He kept fumbling with his worry beads. He had it on like a bracelet around his wrist and he was mumbling some prayers in Greek. Good!! That will keep him focus for a while. As the ambulance pulled into the emergency spot, the doors opened and the paramedic came out. He walked over to our car and said that Shirley was slowing coming around and a bit confused. He asked George to come and fill out some papers the hospital needed.

I peeked into the ambulance and Shirley was semi conscience. She was looking for George and didn't know what happened to her. I reassured her that everything will be clear in a little while and George was here doing paper work with the admission's office.

Poor Shirley, she must be so frightened. As I turned around, Sarge was standing there a little worse for the wear. To be honest I was comforted that I had someone to lean on too. Made me remember how it was to be a couple. I'll try to be nicer to him. At least until I find out what was in that mysterious box.

They admitted Shirley and said she was going to have some tests done and would be a while. George, Sarge and I headed for the cafeteria and tried to digest what just happened and get some food too! I can't believe I could be hungry with all the commotion but I was and I needed some people fuel.

We got some trays and filled them with some soup and sandwiches. As we found a table the nice paramedic that cared for Shirley came over and joined us. His name was Sal and he said he planned on becoming a Doctor. Med school was in September and he spent this gap year going out in the hospital ambulance. He was very positive that Shirley was going to be okay and his initial thought was what I thought too. Shirley was a diabetic. After gaining more than forty pounds her pancreas couldn't keep up with her need for insulin and thus the craving for sweets.

I was glad he came over and George was visibly more relaxed. "My Koukla is going to be Okay?" " She should be fine and if she loses the extra pounds she put on she could probably do without the medication," Sal told us. I think the medical profession will have a very caring and smart young doctor soon. We all wished him good luck with is future as he left to do another call.

Sarge and I left George at the hospital and went back to the vineyard to care for the animals. Our haste to take care of Shirley left the animals unfed and unwatered. Wow, so much for a vacation. I'm already pooped.

#51

Shirley

I think I woke up in a hospital, I had a tube in my nostrils giving me some oxygen, a needle in my arm attached to some kind of fluid. I figured out that it must be a hospital, curtains drawn all around me and when I looked down there was George, head bowed holding my other hand and playing with his Greek beads he wears around his wrist.

"Hi George, what happened? Am I alright"?

"Oh my Koukla, you had me so worried, I am so sorry I ever doubted you. The priest was right. I was jealous of Yia....."

"Whoa George, that's too much information, just tell me why I'm here."

"A little while ago a nice friendly doctor came in to check you. He said you were going to be all right. Said sometimes this happens with people that have gestational diabetes. I was so glad you were going to be all right, I thank him and then sat down and was praying with my worry beads."

"George, what is gestational diabetes? Is there a cure? Why did I pass out?"

"Oh Koukla I was so glad you were going to be Okay I didn't ask. Let me go find Yia Yia, she was a nurse, she should know."

George got up a left in search of Yia Yia, then a perky nurse came in all happy to see I was awake and proceeded to check everything. I was going to ask her but decided to wait to see Yia Yia. Miss Perky told me that every thing looked good and I should be able to go home in a few hours.

I've made a mess of things, I have everyone worried because I can't control my craving for chocolate. I really need a chocolate re-hab.

George is doing his best to make me happy, my best friend is here and this is how I behave. What's wrong with me?

#52
Yia Yia

Sarge and I were sitting in the patient lounge when George ran in and said he needed to talk to me. I got all nervous thinking something was going wrong. Hospitals are no place for sick people. Anyway he was babbling and Sarge sat him down so he could catch himself.

"What's wrong George? Is Shirley going to be ok? What did the doctor say?"

George got a hold of himself and told me that the doctor said Shirley had gestational diabetes and that caused her to pass out. Then he asked what that was?"

"George are you sure that's what he said? Are you positive?" I couldn't believe my ears. I left him with Sarge and went out to the nurse's station. Luckily the young doctor, Sal was writing some orders and looked up when I asked to speak to him.

"I'm Yia Yia, Shirley's best friend and George just told me she has gestational diabetes? Is that correct?"

"Oh yes, that's correct, I ran some test when she was admitted and had a feeling that might the cause of her cravings for sweets, also her husband told me she has put some weight on lately. She's a little old, but I think she will be fine with the proper care," he told me.

Oh my God, who knew? This is a miracle, I asked if I could see her and then thought better of it. I should tell George of this first, he should break the news to her. I was amazed. Wow!!

I hurried back to the patient lounge where George was being comforted by Sarge. Actually I could hardly contain myself. I think I had to be beaming when I came in, the two sad faces in front of me looked so distraught.

" George, get a hold of yourself, I have some exciting news to tell you and then you have to go and see your wife and tell her. Ok? Good!"

George's eye were all teary, Greeks are so emotional. Anyway I proceeded to explain that gestational diabetes happens when a woman gets pregnant, it means that Shirley and you are having a baby!"

With that news George toppled over in a dead faint. We had to get the nurse to bring some smelling salts and revive him.

Sage didn't look so good either. He asked me how old Shirley was and I think she is in her late 40's. Men are so squeamish when it comes to pregnancies.

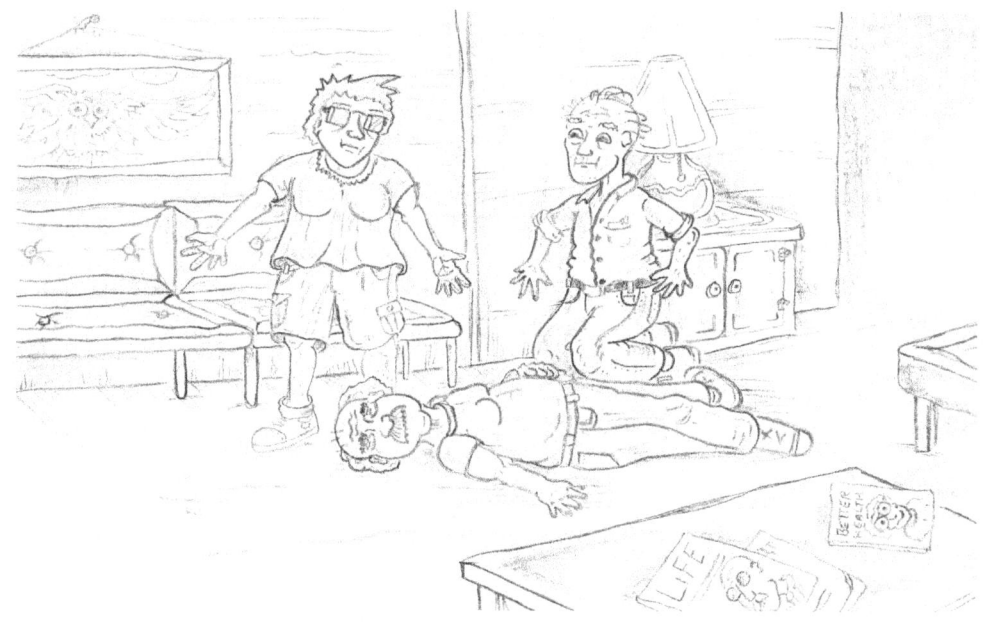

Well, we got George revived and after he realized he was going to be a father he perked right up and was ready to go out and buy cigars.

"Wait a minute George, Shirley doesn't know yet, I think you are the one to tell her."

"Oh no Yia Yia, I need help, I'll tell her but she will want you to share the news, you and Sarge are family, please come with me."

I didn't need to be asked twice, I grabbed Sarge and marched off to see Shirley. Imagine, a new baby. I was a little concerned about the diabetes and Shirley age but I'm sure she'll get great care. Kind of explains the sugar cravings and the weight gain.

Standing outside the drawn curtain in the Emergency room George poked in his head and waved Sarge and me inside her cubical.

George started stammering and couldn't get the words out, he kept staring at Shirley saying Koukla Moo, Koukla Moo.

Shirley was confused her eyes started bulging and she thought something was terribly wrong, I poked George in the ribs and he managed to get the words out. "Shirley my Koukla, we are going to have a baby, a baby!"

Shirley looked over at me and I just nodded, 'Yes!' It was a wonderful moment to share. I know how much Shirley loved kids. She was a great crossing guard and I know this is a very lucky baby to have these two as parents.

Miss Perky nurse said the doctor wanted to do a sonogram; it would be a few more minutes. Sarge and I left Shirley and George alone and went back to the lounge.

Kind of explains things now, the craving, the weight gains; Mother Nature at work.

When we got back to lounge I found Sarge beaming, it was like he was going to be the Daddy. "So what do you think of the news?" I asked.

He said it was terrific, great and he was so happy for both of them; it was like a phoenix rising from the ashes; great now he's all mushy and stuff.

I had a few concerns but I was going to wait a while before I shared them; no sense in ruining everyone's glow.

#53

Sarge

Yia and I left the hospital leaving George alone with Shirley. They admitted Shirley to get her diabetes under control and to give her some educational tools to deal with being diabetic while pregnant.

While understanding about Shirl's age and this complication Yia felt confident that with some help Shirley would be fine. Made me a little troubled about why Yia seemed so quiet and pensive, totally out of character for her.

"So why are you so worried Yia, I thought you said Shirley would be okay?"

"It's not her health that has me so uptight, Sarge. It's me"

I asked her if she was sick and just got a stare and a nod of her head. "What is it Yia? I thought you'd be so happy with the news."

After a few moments she told me. Seems Yia is thinking ahead to her future and decided it wasn't safe to stay at the vineyard. She didn't want to bring any more stress to Shirley and George. Then she really told me her decision. Yia wanted to confront the gang after her and explain how it was Lucey with the nanochips that did them in. She said this vagabond life style wasn't for her, she missed all her family and wanted to go home.

I tried to reason with her about some of the dangerous guys that were looking to silence her. Somehow she didn't want to listen to reason, she felt her presence here put Shirley, George and the unborn child at risk. What could I do? I agreed to contact my superiors, explain the situation and check on the status of the motorcycle gang that was after her.

I was dismayed, at one hand she was miserable leaving her family, and I knew it wasn't in her nature to run from trouble. I suggested we get some rest, I for one was exhausted from all the stress. However I was buoyed about the thought of a new child in our midst. Boy or girl it wouldn't matter, "Let's just have a light supper and a restful evening and make some plans tomorrow Yia, I'm on overload right now. Okay?"

Finally a big smile and a nod of her head; what she did next really surprised me. She wasn't one for spontaneous gestures of affection. But no, she came over to me and rested her head on my shoulders and just gave me a big hug. Next when it was over I caught tears streaming down her face as she went outside to be alone.

From the living room window I watched as she walked to the meadow and brought the two horses into the barn. It was time for them to have some supper and get settled in for the night. Good, I was going to go out and help her but thought better of it. A little alone time for thinking is what she needs now.

I called my boss and told him the situation. He wasn't too please about Yia's decision to face her attackers. I wasn't either. "She's a grown woman, Boss and it bothers her greatly to put other people at risk. Additionally she want Dudley the computer nerd to go with us when we meet the motorcycle guys to explain the chips were transmitting from Lucey the dog not from her."

He told me it was completely up to Dudley, he couldn't force him into a dangerous decision but he assured me he would ask.

"It's all that I can ask for. We will probably be heading back soon, I'll keep you posted as to our plans."

I hung up, thought about it and went outside to give Yia a hand at settling down the horses that and to enjoy the sunset. Life will be taking another twist now. Nothing with Yia around stays the same for long.

#54

Shirley

I'm still in a state of shock with all that's happening to me. I looked over at my hand wondering why I couldn't move it only to see George holding it and his head on the bed. I thought he was sleeping and didn't want to disturb him. I started to pull my hand away so I could sit up only to realize he was just resting.

"Oh sorry George, I just want to go home now, Ok?" "Koukla Moo, anything you want, I'll go get the nurse. They have been so nice here, everyone is so concerned and have taken good care of you. Don't go away, I'll be right back!"

What? With that he ran off and I don't know where he thought I could go, I was tethered to some contraption on my stomach and an IV in my arm and actually I was pretty tired. Men!

Back he came dragging the poor nurse along with him; if it's possible, I swear he was glowing. The nurse came over and told me that I needed to stay at least until tomorrow, that I had an appointment with the Dietician and had to be discharged by the doctor. So she fluff up my pillows, and calmed George down.

He just kept staring at me with big silly grin on his face. "George, let's do as she says. I need to get a lid on all this news, a baby. You and me and a baby we are going to be parents and." Then I got nervous and asked if everything was alright? My age, my addition to chocolate, how can I possibly be OK? Too many things racing around my head, talk about overload. Next I was wondering where Yia Yia was? I needed to talk to her. She'll know what to do? I always envied her with all her Grands, she said they were her happiness. I'm beginning to understand that now, I feel different already.

George told me they went to the vineyard to bed down the horses and get some rest. It was a most unusual day. Wow I'll say!

Can you believe that I am going to be a Mom? I'm old enough to be a Yia Yia although I could never be as, what's the word? Crazy? No, that's not it. Rumbustious? Not that either, I can't think of an adjective that fits so I'll just rest now and maybe it will come to me. Just thinking of being a Mom is enough for now.

#55
Lucey

I was getting a bit worried when Yia and Sarge didn't come back with Shirley. Then I overheard them talking about a baby. OMG… isn't Yia too old? I thought I was her baby, now I have to share with some rug rat? And oh yeah!! They're not even married. I see a shotgun wedding in the near future. What a disgrace in her elder years. You would think she would know better. A baby.

I was sulking around the stable, when Yia brought in the horses from the field. Here I thought Shirley had problems, not even realizing what Yia was going to have, I can't even think of it… a baby. Why couldn't she get a puppy or two? She made sure that I could never get into trouble; she should have gotten spaded too. A baby!

I bet I won't even be allowed to sleep in her big cushy bed anymore. Oh what indignities I suffer.

That's what you get trying to be a sex object: something had to give. I'm going to find that snooty Jack Russell and tell him the news, maybe I can be friends with him and stay here. Shirley always was my best friend, sharing her milk-bones with me, giving me ear scratches. Those were the days. Not like Yia Yia always bossing me around all the time. Her favorite words are 'stop that and cut it out.' Always negative.

Yia was giving the horses some food and humming. Poor kid is going to be subjected to that torture. I wondered where that dog could be? He's not going to like this news either. Maybe I can get him a venerable time and bond. Oh yeah, he's going to subject to my charms and my wily ways.

This news is too much to take I'm going to sulk for the rest of the day. I won't even eat dinner, well maybe a little. Anyway just wait until the Dirty Dozen find out they are going to have a new aunt or uncle. I bet they will be upset too. A baby, yuck!!!

#56

Sarge

While Yia was out taking care of the horses I got a call from George. He told me if everything was okay, that he was going to spend the night with Shirley at the hospital and then the two of them would be home sometime tomorrow. I assured him all was fine and to rest easy, we would talk when he got here.

I can't imagine the mixed emotions they must be having. It's a blessing with so much worry. Poor Yia is so quiet, I worry that she's worrying too. Knowing her she will want to orchestrate everything.

She keeps telling me she's a nurse you know. I try hard not to remind her that it was in the dark ages when they still used leeches and stuff. For that I get a Hrrumph and a nasty look. I'm trying to keep my opinions to myself. Her heart is in the right place; she's just a larger than life character.

Her decision to confront her enemies makes me worried. Sometimes you can't reason with unreasonable people. I called my boss and made him aware of her wanting to leave the protection program and meet with the bikers who wish to do her harm. He was less than enthusiastic. It's a gamble that might not turn out so well, I'll speak to her again after we settle down with this latest news.

Knowing that Shirley would need help and the thoughts of a new child must be swirling around in her head. I know it has me ruffled; a lot to absorb in one day.

George told me that he was renting the vineyard with an option to buy. I doubt he'll want this life style now. Rows and rows of grapes to take care of and then the dependence on Mother Nature for water and sunshine, seems like a gamble to me. It's not my call, but George is a hard worker and an accomplished chef, he has options. We'll see.

I better go out and see of I can help Yia. She's had enough alone time now, time to get back to reality and see if she still wants to go through with facing her foes.

If Dudley the computer guy comes with us I'm sure he would be helpful in explaining the nanochips a lot better than me. I hope I can convince him, he would be putting himself at risk. Never the less, it can't hurt to ask.

#57

Yia

When we got back to the vineyard, I went down to the corral to bring in the horses for the night. I can understand the allure this place has, it is so peaceful and the air is so crisp and clean. Makes me miss the smog. It is hard for me to get my head wrapped around the fact that Shirley is going to be a mom. She'll be great, in some ways she is a child herself. A child like spirit very trusting and warm. Okay, enough of that, let me get to the task at hand.

Rounding up these horses are a lot of work. I sure don't envy doing this for a living. Shirley and George seem to love it, myself I'm more of a city girl. I've been thinking plenty for a while, I am positive now that this is not the way I want to spend my golden years. If Dudley can convince my Biker Boy friends that it was his giving the chips to Lucey and if, that's a big if they believe him, I might get things back to normal.

It's not that I don't appreciate the extra security, but I feel like I am putting all my loved ones at risk. Now with a new baby coming, I sure don't want to bring any trouble to Shirley's doorstep. No, I am going to explain and take my chance. It's the only way to get back to normal, well at least my normal. I know Sarge isn't too happy with my judgment but he needs to get a life too, running around saving me from my enemies can't be easy on an old gopher like him.

Speaking of him, here he comes. He's not a bad sort, just tries to rein in my outgoing spirit sometimes. I don't think he ever relaxes. Not having to worry about me will add years to his life.

"Hi Sarge, you okay? That was some news wasn't it?" "Yia, I'm speechless, too much to absorb today. Thought I come out here and help you with the horses. Maybe later we can talk after dinner. Okay?"

"Sure Sarge, so much going on. I'm pretty tired too. Let's take a night off and talk in the morning. I'm on overload right now and need to wrap my head around all the news of the day."

"Okay Yia, tomorrow will be fine, let's give ourselves a break." So when the horses were fed and blanketed in their stall we headed to the house. I for one was pooped; I looked over at Sarge walking beside me, he was mostly quiet.

I think he disagrees with my plan to talk to the Bikers but this is no life for either of us, I never ran from confrontation and I have to try to get some normalcy back. I hope I can convince him of that.

After a light supper, which consisted of a can of tomato soup and a couple of grilled cheese sandwiches (my favorite) we settled down to watch some TV. Both of us started nodding and got up and called it a night.

What an amazing day. I'm still reliving it as I go to sleep, I remembered to include the new baby in my prayers and wished for it a good, long and happy life. It sure picked some good parents. Well, there's tomorrow and all it brings.

I must have fell off right away. I woke up still achy but raring to go. Long day yesterday and hopefully the excitement will be less today. The weather was co-operating beautifully. I opened the blinds to a shiny bright day that promised to be a 10. As I made my way to the kitchen I realized that Sarge was up already and smelled the coffee waiting for me. Bless him; he had his moments.

"Good morning Sarge, you're up early. Is the coffee ready?" "Hrrumph! I've been up for hours. I couldn't sleep with all the noise coming from the barn. I think the horses sense the stress and are reacting, something has them restless," he replied.

Oh good grief, he's cranky today and here I thought he was being thoughtful; too early in the day to let him sour my mood. No Siree, I was happy and no grouch was going to spoil that.

I didn't ask but suggested we go feed the horses and let them out into the corral. "They probably miss George and Shirley. Animals can sense when things are different," I offered. For that I got another, "Hrrumph!"

I gulped down my coffee, pulled on my boots and made for the door with Sarge behind me. As I said before the day was beautiful. I marveled on how clean the air smelled. Guess the wind was blowing in the right direction, no odors from the barn. Anyway I trudged along Sarge whose legs were longer than mine. Reminded me of when I was little and tried to keep up with my lanky father.

As we entered the barn I saw Mercury all agitated, throwing his head around and stomping his forelegs on the ground. He's mad about something. Then his little stable mate, Barney was all in a lather too. I couldn't imagine what had them so riled up.

Then I saw a bundle of something out of the corner of my eye. At first I wasn't sure then I realized it was a person. An intruder! I quickly alerted Sarge and we cautiously approached the form and to my surprise I recognized him. It was Killer!!

"Killer, what are you doing here? I thought you were a monk now, are you AWOL?" "Yia, is that really you? I never expected to see you in this place? Where's Shirley? " was his weak reply. Sarge didn't give him a chance to explain himself before he grabbed him and took him out of the barn. "You're the reason these animals are so jittery, why are you here?" Sarge wanted to know and know immediately.

"It's a long story and I wish Shirley no harm. You have to understand, she is the most amazing woman I ever met. After I had time to think it over, all I could do was wanting to see her again. The life at the monastery was not for me; all that praying and stuff. Plus they shaved all my hair off the top of my head except for the sides and called me Brother Harry. I found some peace but then I realized that it was just a respite. I need more and the allure of the open road beckoned. You can understand that, can't you Yia?"

Sarge said we had to go back to the house and get this taken care of before George and Shirley came home. I totally agreed and then a light bulb came on and I thought this just could be the ticket back to my old life. Killer knew I would never rat him and the gang out and he was the perfect person to be the go between. Besides, his brother was Turk.

Sarge got into cop mode and had a dozen questions about how Killer knew where Shirley was. That answer was the computer at the monastery. Then he asked about his intentions and told Killer that Shirley was happily married now and pregnant. She needed no excitement and George was a very over protective husband.

Sarge sat and watched Killer absorb all this information and reluctantly Killer said he would do what was right for all. After all, he realized that he was still a half a monk.

My head was twirling with all this. I was planning on taking

Killer back to the gang, have Dudley explain about the nano-chips, and have Killer talk to Turk and voila, the cloud would be lifted. Ah, I envisioned being with the Dirty Dozen again. Making my famous Chicken Soup and oops what about Sarge? I'll worry about him later. Right now I have to plan on going back home and getting on with my life.

Killer had some coffee and then helped with the chores. He seems to have matured a lot since I saw him last. The Sarge was keeping a careful eye on him and Lucey was rolling over for an extra dose of belly rubs.

Chores done, we all walked back to the house and over another cup of coffee and some eggs, I explained why Sarge and I were here; first to see Shirley and George but mostly because I was in the witness protection. I told Bother Harry, aka Killer that I wanted my old life back and asked if he thought he could help me.

"Sure Yia, you have always been a straight arrow with me, I'll speak to Turk and the boys and see what's what. It's probably a misunderstanding. If Dudley swears it was Lucey giving away their location, well maybe they'll… No I'm getting head of myself here. Any eggs left?"

I felt a sense of relief and glanced over to a grumpy Sarge who wasn't buying into this whole plan. Well, it was my choice. So there!

#58

Sarge

I'm not liking this at all; Yia seems to be taken in by in this miraculous appearance of Killer aka Brother Harry or whomever the heck he is. My suspicion gene is working overtime. How exactly did he get here and what does he want? All this goody two shoes doesn't cut ice with me. Somehow I think this was a way to flush Yia out, I could be wrong but the timing fits.

He was wolfing down his third set of eggs and I asked him how he got here, first he said he thumbed his way and then walked the rest. As he got in late he saw the barn and decided to spend the night there. I looked over at Yia and she was all giddy. She thinks he was the answer to all her prayers. I wish I could feel the same. I swore to protect her and I guess these concerns are part of the job.

"You know, so what should I call you anyway? Killer doesn't seem right and Brother Harry isn't it either. So what is it?" "Actually, Sage, my given name is Clarence not one I tell to many people, I think you should just call me Harry, I've been Brother Harry almost three years now," he said.

"So tell me Harry, why did you come here to see Shirley, did you know she was married?" I watched him squirm a bit before he answered." "No Sarge, I hadn't realize she was married, I had a long time to think and she was one of the reasons I joined to Brotherhood. For a while it gave me refuge and comfort, but nobody talked, all they did was pray and pray some more. Actually, I'm all for praying, but I just felt there was more in life for me. I started thinking and realized that Shirley was the reason I left the gang and decided on a different path. She scared me straight so to speak. I wish her no harm only good things. I will leave before she arrives, I have no intentions of giving her more concerns."

I'm trying to decide if this guy is for real. He talks a good job but I'm not letting my guard down. No Siree. Yia is all elated thinking of a normal life surrounded by her Dirty Dozen. I need to do a little more interrogation and a place to stash him for a while.

I asked him to help me with the morning chores, which he took to right away. He fed and groomed the horse and led them to pasture. Seems he knows his way around a farm.

Meanwhile I found a cheap motel not far from here where I will park him until I call my boss and set up some sort of meeting. I am still worried about this. I can't talk to George he gets too emotional and I don't think he wants Mr. Harry hanging around Shirley anyway. I know I wouldn't.

After lunch Shirley was being discharged from the hospital and Yia is going to pick them up and bring them home. Yia Yia agreed that we had to stash Harry someplace for a while and then decide what the next plan would be. Yia suggested that Harry might be helpful when she meets with the Bikers. Harry is Turk's brother. I didn't know that. I don't know exactly what Yia is planning but she is determine to get this clock of suspicion off her shoulders and resume her life of annoying everyone she can; my thoughts, not hers.

I'm taking Harry to the motel and get him set up and then Yia is going to pick up Shirley and George. She plans on telling them tonight that we are leaving and she's going to try to get her old life back. Interpreted that means she plans to come back when all is settled and totally spoil this new infant. I guess it will be the Dirty Dozen plus one. I'm keeping my fingers crossed this works out well, that's not to say I'm not nervous about the decision.

Well, I took Harry to town, got him some toiletries and a change of clothes. I bought him some snacks and gave him some money to call for pizza later. That should take care of things for a while. In the meantime Yia left to get Shirley and George. It's time to tell them we have to go. I have a call through to my boss and hope he can get us out here as soon as he can. Everyday with Harry around makes me nervous. Yia is a happy as can be, thoughts of resuming her old life and totally annoying everyone is making her giddy.

#59

Lucey

Er, wait a minute. What? I don't get any of this. First Shirley eats too much chocolate and now she's pregnant? No wonder they won't let dogs have any chocolate, it's the human form of doggie birth control. I'm beginning to get the drift. But now Shirley is going to have one of those rug rats probably from all that chocolate she's been chowing down. I'm starting wonder where I fit into that equation; will she'll still eat milk bones and romp around with me? Please, she was my only bright spot in a life full of Don'ts! It's a cruel, cruel world!

Now their conversations I have been overhearing has her (Yia) wanting to get out of the witness protection program. In one way I don't care, but what if someone takes a shot at her and hits me my mistake. I vote no! Life here is not bad. Lots of room and the Jack Russell is warming up to my charms. However those horses are mighty large, those I could do without. In this place I don't even need a leash, I roam around at will, that's the life of a country dog. Yeah, it really has advantages.

I vote we stay. If that Killer didn't show up I bet we would be here longer. I'm sure I'll get dragged all over the place again. Good thing I'm flexible. Car and trains and planes, even boats; amazing, I'm a world traveler with four legs. I have to remember to put that on my resume.

I think that maybe they (Sarge &Yia) should leave me here. I can cuddle up next to Shirley and relax her by letting her pet me. Oh yeah! See I'm still a therapy dog; that training never leaves plus the fact that I am so great at it; oh yeah! I have to figure out a way for Yia to leave me behind. Maybe I can get lost when they're ready to go, or maybe pretend I'm sick. I have to come up with a plan; don't worry, I'm good.

Next I'm going to see what they're doing now; maybe take a stroll around the hood. I am torn between wanting to stay here and my responsibilities of taking care of poor old Yia Yia. I thought it over, Let's see, I think I'll stay here. Shirley may need a hand in teaching the rug rat how to be nice to dogs. Particularly moi!

#60

Yia Yia

My mind is made up! I'm going back to my home and straightening out the claims against me. I have been wrongly accused of narcing. I've never narced in my life and well that's a long time. Don't ask.

Sarge is less than convinced but I think with Killer coming with us and Dudley explaining it was Lucey, I can't see why they would still want to harm me. Plus I can trade Killer for me. Yeah, seems I have a few hands to play. I'll pressure Sarge to get us on a plane, not that I like to fly, but time is a wasting and I don't want the Dirty Dozen to grow up with out my guidance.

Sarge was supposed to get hold of his boss to make arrangement for our return. I wonder what's become of him. We have to leave and pick up Shirley and George in a few minutes. He's not too keen on returning and I think Killer has freaked him out somewhat. Not everyday you get a second chance, this is mine and I have to make the most out of it.

I hope Shirley doesn't mind but I will ask her to watch Lucey until I get this all settled. If things don't work out well, anyway Lucey seems to like it here. It's hard on Lucey with all this confusion, I hate to admit it, and she's getting up in age too! Then if they what revenge on Lucey I can just tell them she is in doggie heaven already. Yeah that should be the ticket.

Got the horses outside, that big black stallion is in a sour mood.

Reminds me of cranky Sarge at suppertime. Must be a male thing. I haven't time to worry on it now. Sarge went to check on Killer and he's running late, I'm sitting here ready when he comes back. Sure hope Shirley is okay, I know how much she loves chocolate but she'll have to watch her diet closely from now on. I am still reeling that she's going to have a baby. Oh, life sure does throw out surprises.

Here he comes now, I am so eager to get Shirley now and make her a big bowl of my famous chicken soup. It's on the stove now and almost finished.

Oh good! Sarge is ready, I turned off the soup and anxious to get Shirley back home. I'll explain my plans in the car. I'm sure she will be nervous a bit but she'll understand. I hope.

Sarge came in all flustered and said to give him about an hour. He had some important things to take care of first and then we'll go pick-up the Mama to be and George. It's okay gives me more time to finish the soup and get my support hose on. Sometimes it takes a lot of jumping up and down to get those things up onto this aging body.

#61

Sarge

I've been in touch with my boss checking on Brother Harry. This whole thing just doesn't sit well with me. I don't believe in coincidences and Brother Harry showing up and oh so ready to help straighten things out, smells to the high heavens to me. Yia is just so trusting that she is ready to go back into a trap. That's my take on this whole thing. No sense in trying to convince Yia of that. She's in protective Mom mode and wants to make sure that Shirley hasn't got any danger around her.

My boss suggested and I agreed that the best way to handle this is for Brother Harry to disguise himself as Yia Yia and travel with me to New York. There we will convince Dudley the nerd to come with us when we meet up with the gang. Hopefully Dudley can then convince them that it was Lucey transmitting their whereabouts and not Yia. Returning Harry will be a show of good faith. Sounds a little sketchy to me but its all we have to offer. I haven't told Harry these plans yet, it will be interesting to see how he reacts. I still am not comfortable with his miraculous appearance.

After putting Yia on hold in the morning I went over to talk to Harry about my plan. He was up and about and said he just got back from having breakfast. I told him I wanted him to disguise himself as Yia Yia and he and I would travel to see the gang and get this whole misunderstanding straightened out.

At first he looked at me as if I was speaking Greek. Then the light bulb popped over his head and he said he'd do anything I thought would help. He also said he had wanted to return to the East and see all his old pals. He snickered about returning as a white haired old lady.

Not taking any chances of leaving him alone to inform someone of my plan I told him we had to leave immediately. "Fine with me, let's go," was his reply.

We stopped at a wig store where I bought Harry a short white wig and then onto the shoe store for a pair of woman's sneakers. I was racking my brain on what else he needed? Well, after we picked up a few items, we went back to the vineyard to tell Yia of the plan. I'm sure I'll meet some resistance there but I think this will keep her safe until I can get an understanding with the motorcycle gang and get the hit removed.

Our plane is nonstop and we have an afternoon flight. We'll be met at the airport by some undercover guys and taken to a safe location. Can't say I'm not worried. Convincing Dudley to co-operate is another obstacle to over come.

It will be all so worth it if this goes as planned. We all can get on with our lives and I can finally give Yia the box she's so eager to receive. My biggest problem next is getting Yia to understand and have patience. She likes being in charge of everything. This time she will have to play it cool and wait for me to get some results.

#62
Brother Harry

I was wondering how I was going to get to New York and then like a miracle, Sarge tells me I am going there with him. The downsize is I have to dress up like that old lady Yia Yia and pretend on the flight that I have a cold and wear a face mask or something like that. I can't wait to see Turk and all my old friends. I really miss them. I know I didn't have the same bad boy personality as they do, but they were all I knew growing up. If it weren't for Shirley scaring me stupid I would still be riding with them. What a woman!!

No sense in me hanging around here, I was grateful that Turk told me where she was but I didn't have the courage to face her. Funny how things work out: now she's going to be a Momma and I get to go and see the gang and my brother.

Sarge took me to a wig store and then off for some sneakers. I sure hope I don't have to wear a dress. I refuse to shave my legs, deal or no deal. Our plane leaves at one PM and arrives in New York around nine PM. At least that's what Sarge told me.

Tomorrow we are supposed to meet with some computer geek and then hook up with the bikers who are not doing time. I tried to get more info out of Sarge but we're not the best of buds, I think he eyes me suspiciously. I'll do my best to make him more comfortable around me, I can't be any worse than the old woman he drags everywhere.

As I sat waiting for Sarge to pick me up my thoughts drifted to Shirley and my first ride with her. She came to the used car lot with her friend Yia Yia. Next thing I know Turk told me to take Shirley for a ride, he had business to discuss with Yia Yia. I hopped on the nearest bike and Shirley jumped on and grabbed me around my waist. Together we went flying out of the yard and onto the local highway. She sure was a good sport and I was already smitten. Somewhere along the way she pleaded with me to drive, I was skeptical at first, no girl ever drove me around. What could I do? I couldn't deny this Princess anything.

She was fantastic, little did I know she was a stuntwoman and I was in for the ride of my life. It was long before my enthusiasm turned into sheer terror. She was jumping lanes, heading for oncoming trailers, speeding like a bullet and I was hanging on for dear life. Lucky for me we needed gas and when we stopped to fill up I got off the bike and ran into the bathroom. I had the poop scared right out of me. I prayed very hard in there and promised to turn my life into something good if only God would spare me.

Shirley knocked and asked me to come out and that's when I told her I would when Hell freezes over. Well, she said she couldn't wait that long and left without me. My prayers were answered.

Try as I might I still carry a soft spot for her. She's amazing, fearless and sweet all at the same time: that George is one lucky man.

I wish them many wonderful years and I thank her for me finding Jesus. It would have never happened if it weren't for Shirley.

As I was basking in my reverie I heard Sarge pull up. Showtime I guess. I'm lucky to get this free trip to New York. I was wondering how I was going to get there and now this plan. I don't mind impersonating Yia Yia; the boys will get a kick out of it, I'm sure.

#63
Sarge

Well, I'm as ready as I'm going to be. I feel somewhat nervous leaving Yia alone without me. George swore to me that he will keep a careful eye out for her and try to curtail her the best he can. Good luck with that. Time to get Harry and set up the meeting with the bikers. I am hoping that bringing Harry back and if Dudley can convince them it was Lucey transmitting their where abouts maybe we can all get on with our lives. I don't blame Yia for wanting out, this is no way to spend her golden years.

I got some of Yia's clothes and her old trench coat; that should be enough of a disguise. I just have to get Harry to shuffle a little so he seems a bit older. I was going to ask him to wear a Kevlar vest but I think it would freak him out, so I decided to keep mum about it.

The plan is set for Yia (Harry) and me to board early in the first class area and keep a low profile. As for exiting the craft, we would be the last to leave with the crew and met by an unmarked car. In the morning we will pick up Dudley, who agreed to set the record straight and proceed to an undisclosed location. Hopefully this meeting will clear this matter up and Yia can go back to being Yia and the world will be a better place. Yadda Yadda.

Personally, I don't have much faith in the promises of this biker crowd, I think it is a mistake but it's a chance we have to take.

Bringing Harry back and the word of Dudley the nerd is thin. I'm going to keep my fingers crossed and follow my instincts.

Harry has been extremely co-operative and can't wait to see his old friends. Sometimes he seems too good to be true. I guess it's my cop personality that makes me suspicious. Well, I'm going to throw the dice and hope for the best.

After supper, we will say our goodbyes and settle down for our trip in the AM. I'm a little nervous about leaving Yia behind. George promised me he'd would be on guard but leaving him with the two women to watch, it's a lot to ask. I'll hurry back as soon as I can.

Yia was particularly quiet through out dinner and definitely had something weighing on her mind. I waited until we were alone and asked her what was troubling her. She said she wanted to go with us in the morning, that she should talk to the bikers herself. Actually,. She was worried about being a danger to Shirley and was hesitant to tell me that she was losing her security blanket, me!!

Well, I'll be. The woman never seemed to notice I was around, she sure can have her tender moments. I tried to convince her this was the safest and best was to handle this situation and explained all the things that were set up. It wasn't much of an appeasement but she said she understood, didn't entirely agree, but understood. I promised as soon as the meeting was over that I would call and let her know everything that went on and my opinion.

She agreed and gave me a peck on my cheek and left me sitting on the porch looking out on the bucolic countryside. It's hard to believe that this peace comes with such a heavy price.

Early the next day Brother Harry, disguised as Yia Yia and I left for the plane. I tried to pry some information out of him but he just said he was out of the picture for so long that I probably know more than he does. We were whisked to out first class seats and Harry quickly pulled down his hat and snoozed away. Nothing seems to bother him much. I can't help but be concerned leaving Yia and although George means well, he's not a policeman. I have to take it on faith. Maybe Brother Harry can share some of his.

Before long the plane started up and we were headed to the Big Apple. Dudley agreed to meeting with the Biker Gang and plans to tell how the cookies were given to the dog, Lucey without Yia's knowledge. It's a shot we have to take so Yia can resume her life and I can move on with mine. We hit some turbulence and when I looked over at Harry I realized he was praying. This guy has me confused.

Upon landing we waited until the plane emptied of passengers and then joined the crew on their vehicle back to the hanger. There waiting for us was an unmarked police car. We spent the night at a safe house and in the morning we are going to hook up with Dudley and then go meet a representative of the biker club at an undisclosed location. All this cloak and dagger stuff caused by one white haired old lady. Glad she couldn't hear me, I'd get clobbered.

Anyway, I was hoping for a positive ending. Bringing Harry back and Dudley explaining how he fed the nanochips to the dog, well it might just work.

#64

Brother Harry

I can hardly wait to see my brother; it seems like forever. We grew up on the streets, I didn't know my Dad and my Mom well, she had issues so Turk, my big brother mostly took care of me. I wasn't as tough as him, he surely handled himself and then some. I'm thinking I still have to find my way back to the monastery, maybe Sarge with bring me back when this meeting is over.

I'm really nervous about this, I know running off and becoming a monk wasn't in Turks ideal vocation for me. It wasn't until I thought I was going to die on the back of that bike that I realized I had to do something good with my life. I hope he understands and respects that. Sarge and that crazy old woman he protects, well he has his hands full. Keeping her alive should be a punishment enough. I really wanted to see Shirley again, but knowing she's happy and now going to be a Mom that's such a nice blessing for her. Something has to calm her down unless she gets a wild child like her. Heaven forbid.

It's almost time to leave, we're being driven there with Dudley and then we go to an undisclosed location. A lot of cloak and dagger, but that's how Turk operates. He likes the drama.

Dudley seems a bit on edge, I wish I could reassure him but I really don't know how this plays out. He brought along some of the chips he fed the dog hoping to be able to explain how they work. I admire his bravery for coming, he didn't have to, I am praying for him to be successful.

Finally we reach our destination; a broken down warehouse on an abandon pier near the Hudson River. It doesn't seem like anyone is here. We all got out cautiously and entered the old building that smelled of mold and had mice and rat droppings all over. We were ushered into a room at the back which was pretty nice, good furniture and some coffee brewing. I was overwhelmed when I saw my brother. I had a million questions to ask but at that moment all I need was a big hug.

Finally things quieted down and I asked where Rocco was? "Oh Rocco, he stepped down. I'm in charge now. Your big brother is in charge," he said that with pride and a big smiley face.

I hope that is a good thing, anyway the Sarge said, "Let to get down to business. I understand there is a contract on Yia Yia's life, I want to know how we can resolve this peacefully without anyone getting rubbed out." Turk spoke up right away and said that he knew Yia would never rat them out, she had more than one opportunity and she would never blew the whistle. As far as he was concerned she was aces. That what he said, "aces."

That didn't satisfy the Sarge who said word on the street was that you were looking for retribution and she was going to get it.

Turk replied," Sarge, Sarge Sarge, you got it all wrong, the real culprit is the fink who fed the dog the chips, that's who we want. Flushing him out has been hard but eventually we'll get him.

Oh no, we took Dudley right into a trap, Dudley just sat there frozen and paralyzed with fear. Then Turk when went on to say that they wanted Dudley to work for them, if they could feed their competition the chips they would get the low down on all the plans the other gangs have for the waterfront. It seemed they didn't suspect Dudley was the Nanochip giver. He walked over and gave Dudley a big slap on the back. Dudley smiled weakly and at that point needed smelling salts.

"So, Yia Yia was just the bait to get you guys the ammo you need for the operations?" said Sarge.

"Sure, I never would hurt that sweet old lady, she makes the best chicken soup ever. Actually we almost lost her once, but she showed her true colors at the police station when none of the tellers refused to ID her. She's our secret weapon, Turk sounded so sincere.

It was time for me to speak up, "Turk, you are my big brother, and I love you more than anyone on this earth, but I cannot allow you to hurt anyone, anymore. You need to let bygones be bygones." With that Turk turned to me and said he couldn't believe that I was really a monk, a man of peace. How did that happen? He was grooming me to be his right hand man.

"It's a calling Turk, I'm even surprised myself, but I never felt more at peace and I have serenity in my life that I never knew existed. Maybe you can come back with me and try it for yourself. Let all this other stuff go, life is too short and shorter still with your lifestyle."

I looked over and saw that Dudley had passed out, Sarge was bug eyed and Turk, well he was just staring at me, open mouth.

Then Turk came over to me and said, "Just this one time Harry, I'm letting it all go, if you are truly happy I can ask for no more. Go with these guys and live your peaceful life. I will seek no retribution, seeing you so strong and dedicated to your beliefs has touched a part of me that I never knew existed. Now get these guys out of here before I change my mind." I gave him a giant hug and knew I would probably never see him again. From that moment on I belonged to God.

#65

Sarge

I am skeptical. It was too easy, all of a sudden everything goes away? I think there is another motive at work here. After we revived Dudley, we got back in the car and I watched as Turk and Harry said their 'goodbyes,' If something is too good to be true, it's too good to be true.

I promised Yia I would call her after the meeting. I'm not sure on what to tell her. It seemed clear to me that Yia Yia was acting like bait for the gang, but that was much too easy. Poor Dudley may never be the same, he thinks he's a marked man and he's probably right.

I've got to think this over and discuss it with my boss. Maybe he can make some sense of it. Yia never told or ratted their gang out, that's true. Perhaps they were looking for the way we knew where they were. Most of them did very little time for the bank job but some had outstanding warrants and went to jail. If they didn't want to do the time they should have done the crime. Right?

Arriving back at the house we sat around thinking of the days events. After calling Yia Yia, she was overcome with glee thinking she could go back to her old life of spoiling the Dirty Dozen and was impatiently waiting for Shirley's new baby. That poor child will have Yia Yia on it like white on rice. I think all these kids give her life meaning and fill her with happiness. I hope there is some room left for me.

Anyway, getting back to today, it was very peculiar that Turk took all the news especially that Harry wanted to return to the monastery and that Turk really meant no harm to Yia Yia. Dudley definitely doesn't want to work for the gang but I think bringing Dudley with us to that meeting put a face on the one who gave the dog the chips. I think that Dudley is correct in assuming he's a marked man.

Oh the plot just gets thicker and it's hard to tell who is pulling whose chains. One thing for sure, I think that gang wants to send a message and needed to clear up who gave the dog the chips. I'm should have figured that out. I'm an idiot. Looking back we played right into their hands, Drat!

I spoke it over with the Captain and he came up with a plan to protect Dudley. Said Dudley was a lifelong bachelor and would be able to relocate without too much hassle. Plans were made to get him plastic surgery, have him grow a small mustache and beard and then give the old Dudley a mock funeral. Hopefully it will satisfy the gang who want him dead and give Dudley a new beginning. Meanwhile, he said my job was to bring back Yia so she can resume her life and thanked me for my part in this camouflage.

Preparations were made for me to get Harry and me back to the vineyard and for Harry to return to the monastery. Somehow I still can't believe that he is for real. Seems too easy but I guess stranger things have happened. Who am I to doubt the Gods?

#66

Yia Yia

Finally a word from Sarge; he told me that the motorcycle gang used me to flush out the person who fed Lucey the Nanochips. Once they knew it was Dudley they weren't interested in me anymore. How rude!!

Anyway, I can go home again and I promised Shirley and George that they can stay with me until George finds himself a new place or gets a job. Not that I wish him a hard time but I really would love for that baby to be born near me. Taking his time would be a blessing for me.

I'm thinking since the gang was trying to find out the fink that gave Lucey the chips, that once they did they lost interest in me means I can go back to my home and normal life. Just wondering now if it will include Sarge? I kind of got used to him being around, I guess I will have to wait for Sarge to get back before any decision is made, waiting is difficult for me.

Meanwhile, Shirley is glowing more each day and I think I saw an extra swagger in George's walk: why not with such a surprise. Shirley is eating properly and getting her rest. In fact I think George and I have become annoying to her.

I finally heard from Sarge and he should be here tomorrow. Brother Harry is returning to the monastery and Sarge and I will spend a few extra days here before I get back to the Dirty Dozen and make my famous Chicken Soup.

Part of me can't wait to go back and the other part wants to stay. Too many decisions to make and I haven't had my fill of the tranquility this place offers. Life goes on and so in a few days I go back and resume spoiling my Dirty Dozen. I miss them terribly too! So, mixed emotions at play.

Time to go bring in Mercury, the big black stallion that seems to know everything but is so stoic. Yeah, animals know. I lead him into his stall and give him his bag of oats. We've become fast friends and I will miss his gentle courage and strength. A gentle giant.

#67

Sarge

I've made our travel arrangements and we will be back home in a few days. At least Yia is out of the witness protection and can go back to her normal zany life. I'm hoping it will include me. I still have the box with me and I think maybe I should give it to her before we leave. She might want to share her news, good or bad with Shirley.

Thinking about it over and over, well, I know it's iffy but if she'll have me, I still would like to be married to her. She is certainly a handful but has a good heart. Not too many people fill that bill. I spoke to George for his opinion and he encourages me to go for it. Said it was the best thing he ever did and now he's going to be a Papa. I am so happy for him. I think he has been given a blessing that he acknowledges with grace. Good man, George.

Brother Harry has returned to the Monastery and is more certain that he has chosen his life's work. I had a hard time trying to decide if he was for real, guess it's my cop's nature to be wary of things being too good to be true. Shirley sure gave him a different point of view of life on that memorable ride.

Tonight after supper just as the sun starts to set, I think I will give Yia the box. I am so nervous. What if she turns me down? Then what? It will probably end our friendship, oh what a dilemma!

There is a tree just about on the edge of the property that I think is a perfect place to walk to after dinner. Listening to the crickets and frogs making noise that will be my orchestra. Beats violins any day.

I was so nervous at supper I could hardly eat. Yia didn't miss much and asked me if I felt okay? I said I just think I need some fresh air and asked her to take a walk with me. "Just go relax a minute while I tidy up the kitchen, then I'll be all yours."

If only I were that lucky!!

#68

Yia Yia

I wonder if Sarge is okay? He hardly touched his supper and if I say so myself, it was stupendous. I made Shirley's favorite chicken and rice, fresh greens from the garden and homemade apple pie for dessert. If I wasn't watching my girlish figure I'd have two pieces of pie, but I restrained myself.

Could be Sarge is tired; barely said anything at dinner. I guess the strain of the past few days is catching up to him. A nice walk in this beautiful land will be just the ticket. I am going to miss this place but wanting to see my family will take the sting out. Can't wait to give each of them a big hug and sloppy kiss.

Dishes done and Shirley all propped up watching TV, I grabbed a sweater and told Sarge I was ready. He was fussing with something, gave George a wink and off we went. Outside the earth at sunset has the sweetest smell; it's just so, so earthy. I'm glad for this stroll and some time to talk. Of course, Sarge not being a man of many words, meant I had to drag everything out of him. I think he has had a rough couple of days trying to get all my problems and Brother Harry's problems and Shirley and George's problems all taken care of before we returned home. He takes his job so seriously. Perhaps that's what draws me to him. His strength.

We walked passed the grape vines down to an open meadow. There by a big sprawling maple tree, he stopped and fumbled around in his pocket. Now what?

As I admired the view and the peace that it brought, Sarge interrupted my reverie by handing me the box. THE BOX? THAT BOX!!!

I stared at it then at him and hesitantly took it. I've wondered for like forever about it and here it was. In MY HAND!

I was so nervous that I could hardly take off the wrapping, I handed it back to him for help and he thought I didn't want it. "No Sarge, just take off the wrapping. I'm so nervous I can't"

A ring box for sure, I watched a he carefully took off the bow, then the paper. He opened it and got down on his creaky one knee and looked up to me. "Yia I would be honored if you would take this and promise to be my wife."

I took the box and inside was the prettiest diamond ring, a perfect solitaire mounted on gold. The prettiest ring in the world came attached to Sarge and a promise to share my life with him.

Removing the ring out of the box I handed it to Sarge, he gave me a quizzical look as I extended my hand for him to put it on my finger. I tried to speak but I was too emotional. We sealed the deal with a kiss and a hug and nary a word was said. What do you say?

We lingered until sunset and then went back to the house to share our good news with Shirley and George.

Yep, I was going to be Mrs. Sarge!!!

Our Book Club

I dedicated this book to a fine bunch of women who welcomed me warmly into their Book Club and have touched my life in many different and wonderful ways.

My daughter Pat took me along one fateful evening and ever since my life has been enriched by the sharing of theirs. Although by no means are the books we read are the main reason, I think it's their friendship and wine that we really seek.

A diverse group, professional and businesswomen, assorted ages and religions, a mini United Nations of sorts; we meet once a month to discuss the selection. Aided by questions regarding the book of choice we muddle through and then are treated to that evening's selection of delicious and calorie laden treats.

There is hardly a meeting where all 12 of us have read the book completely but there is no penalty's given.

So thanks'once again Ladies for your friendship and hospitality; you have enriched and expanded my mind and my waist line.

What follows are some minutes of our get togethers. Hope you enjoy reading them and bear in mind that I haven't lost mine. (Mind that is)

Pat aka Yia Yia

MORE

MORE

MORE

The folowing is some minutes written with tongue in cheek of some of our meetings. Just my over active imagination at work and how Blessed I am my Book Club buddies have a sense of humor.(I hope)

MORE........

Hi Kids,

I know it's not camp time, but I had to write and tell you about the most interesting day I had.

With two of my friends, Cathy and Jo, we boarded the Rocketship and took off for the Big Apple, that's New York City. Our destination was the Museum of Modern Art, it was exhibiting the works of Vincent Van Gogh.

You have to have your folks take you there it's a most awesome place.

All started out fine cruising along Route 80 heading for the George Washington Bridge. On the scan and going across, Cathy began obsessing about a little red lighthouse at the New York's side base. Cathy was doing her best to get us to look at the lighthouse, at that time the rocket ship was cruising at 70 MPH and on the curvy exit ramp. Being the good pilot I kept my eyes on the road with the exception of glancing in the back at Jo rolling her eyes. The in unison we both said, "Oh yeah, it's sooo cute!" That satisfied Cathy and we continued to speed merrily along.

Once off the West Side Highway we traveled crosstown in the usual chaotic New York traffic. Crazy cabs, delivery boys on bikes weaving in and out of vehicles, buses pulling out in front of you without looking, pedestrians daring you to hit them, the usual stuff.

Cathy seemed to blanch a little and her knuckles were turning white on the suicide handle. "You sure know your way around," she said. "Well, that's because I learn to drive in the city, " I replied smugly. Jo said nothing, she was too busy with her prayer beads.

We made it to our destination in no time and after docking the rocket ship we ventured to the museum's entrance. The line of art lovers was probably a mile long. Your Yia Yia, (moi) being a member flashed my card and we were admitted right away.

Fate was smiling on us that day because a woman we didn't know came up to us and gave us three free tickets to the exhibit. Just like that!

Wow, our lucky day, we all planned to by lottery tickets when we got home.

We proceeded to the exhibit, which had another long line but armed with my trusty membership card we barged right in. With luck like this we are sure to hit the megamillions.

I got a little woozy, my old nemesis, Mr. Bad Ear showed up and I went outside to sit down for a few minutes. Super sleuth Jo figured me gone and came out to find me. I convinced her I was okay but she said to stay put and went back in to get Cathy. Cathy arrived and immediately opened her pocketbook. Inside look like a miniature Walgreens. Man she had everything in there. As I peered into that abyss I thought I saw a bottle of Jamisons; maybe not. Anyway, she fixed me up with some kind of powerful mint and I was back to normal in no time.

The girl guarding the door tried to prevent us from going back in but Cathy convinced her that I had all the tickets and the Jo, Cathy and I rushed the door. There was no stopping us! Talk about women on a mission!!

The Van Gogh paintings were totally amazing, truly something you all should see someday. We enjoyed our time there and the reconnected out of the exhibit space to formulate our next move. On to the modern sculpture show; some pretty weird things in there for sure.

There was a Con Edison man hole cover, a bike rack a wall hanging of a large Brill-O pad, soil erosion mats, broken pottery chandeliers just to name a few.

Cathy saw an unusual lounge chair and she had a flashback of a certain red chair she called "the Animal" a holdover from her hippy days. Her reminiscing made her eyes glaze over and a goofy smile appeared on her face. She must of read a lot of good books while reclining on the chair. Again, Jo just rolled her eyes.

Next stop was the photography gallery. Photos and history from the time the things were invented up to present day. Among the interesting photos was one large blow up of a woman's legs. Cathy claimed it was her legs. Jo just kept rolling her eyes.

Well, all this viewing makes a person hungry; it was time to get something to eat. We all decided to check out the Museum's Café. After blindfolding Cathy, Jo and I guided her over the divide separating the floors. Cathy gets vertigo and we were afraid she might leap over the balcony and who knows what she was nipping from her bag.

The café's price list was like the National debt but we thought we were going to hit it big with the lottery so we all decided to go for it. However the chow line was out the wahoo, we could barely see the salamis and cheeses hanging in the far distance. We were way too hungry to wait and my card had lost it's magic. A unanimous decision was made to take our chances on the streets of New York.

After walking and circling four city blocks then getting weak from hunger I was ready to settle for a dirty water hot dog. This time both Cathy and Jo rolled their eyes.

Plan B went into action and we decided to return to the Garden State to seek our sustenance there. Back in the Rocketship with more white knuckles and praying we were on the West Side highway in no time. Speeding towards the GW Bridge we all saw the little red lighthouse and then there was peace upon the land.

Your Yia Yia was appointed team leader and given the job of deciding where to go. I chose my favorite Chinese restaurant I knew in Fore Wee.

We were all getting giddy from hunger and I could feel myself losing strength, just a little further to go. Finally we reached our destination and after docking the Rocketship we all alit and ran to the restaurant. Well, not really ran, we had to climb over some dirty snow mounds the size of Mt. Everest first.

Salvation was in sight. As we settled into our table, Cathy excused herself and left the table with her pocketbook and headed to the restroom. She came back looking happy. I should have gone with her. I could use some happy too!

Anyway, I had to help the girls out; they had a hard time making a decision. Lack of blood sugar for sure! As team leader I took charge and ordered. Now we waited anxiously for our foods arrival. Ah, the pleasure of a steaming bowl of wonton soup. It had something strange shredded on it. We didn't care. They gave us only one spring roll which we divided into there, we didn't care. Then two Bar-be-Que spareribs for the three of us, a bit tricky, but we didn't care. We were all mellow and contemplating hitting the big bucks tonight.

After paying our check we went outside, a sinking feeling came over me. The Rocketship was missing!! OH NO!!

While we were perusing the area a half man, half ape came over to us. He said he was the security guard from the bank. Yeah,…right! Apeman said we were in the restaurant since one thirty PM and we illegally parked Blah, Blah, Blah!!

Interpreted it meant they towed the Rocket. Fate has turned her back on us. How cruel!

We looked around the parking lot and saw a multitude of signs.

They must have been erected as we were eating. Indeed it said that illegally parked cars would be towed. The indignity of this! We all proceeded to the bank; me to the ATM and Cathy and Jo to assault the bank president.

I retrieved some cash and called for a cab to take us to the place where they took the Rocketship. When I look for Cathy and Jo, Cathy had the bank's president with his arms behind his back and Jo had her rosary beads wrapped around his neck. He was sputtering and crying out for mercy.

Onlookers were cheering and egging Cathy and Jo on, I too would have strangled him but the cab was coming and convinced Cathy and Jo to feed him to the angry mob that gathered.

A taxi pulled up, it looked like a reject from the Rent-a-Dent company. Inside was a driver who was wearing a roach motel around his neck. Cathy and Jo quickly jumped into the back seat leaving me to get in the front. Cowards!!

I couldn't help myself I asked the driver if he lost his razor. His white bristly beard was shaggy and surreal. On impulse I touched it to see if it came off (I thought maybe he was a left over Santa Claus.) Totally annoyed he threatened to throw me out of the cab. I was tempted to ask if he was getting enough fiber, but I could see he had no sense of humor. He then told us that he hasn't shaved since the Vietnam days; from the look of him he hasn't bathed either.

Luckily we made it to the car lot and there looking sad and lonely was the Rocketship. The girls insisted on paying some of the ransom and we all piled in after securing its release.

Traveling back home, it was noted that Happy Hour was upon us, so one last stop at my place for a glass of wine to end our adventure. Lucey was overwhelmed to see so many people to jump on. She outdid herself with greetings.

I showed the girls my letters that I send to my Grands at camp. Cathy said she wrote some nonsense to her kids too. Then we hatched a plan to do the Grandma Chronicles. At our next Book Club meeting we are going to get every grandma on board and make ourselves a book.

After that we mused over how fate changed from smiling to turning her back on us. There will be no lottery tickets today. But we were safe, I don't know how sound but we were ready to embark on another escapade in the spring. Proving you just can't keep a Good Grandma down!!

MORE...... X's 2

Hi Kids,

Just a note to keep you posted on my doings; I know you are always interested in my adventures. Well, this isn't an adventure but it sure is fun. I belong to a Book Club that Aunt Pat introduced me to, I think she bribed some members to let me in. However she did it I am very thankful,

Our Book Club is a group of about 12 members, all ladies of mixed ages and occupations. Our meetings are on a rotation basis, someone volunteers to have the next one and provides the eats and drinks. We have lively and interesting conversations and sometimes it is actually about the assigned book of the month. With me so far?

Last night our meeting was at Alicia's house, she's a lawyer. Aunt Pat picked me up and we traveled over snowy and icy roads to our destination.

Snowy and icy doesn't begin to describe Alicia's driveway. It looked like the expert run at Vermont's Mt. Snow. An official looking man was at the base holding a clipboard. He told us the T-Bar was out of order and we had to sign a waiver of liability before proceeding at our own risk. Everyone before us signed; amazing the allure of free eats and drinks.

After signing we made our ascent reaching the summit as we struggled through the ice-laden overgrowth to Alicia's massive front door. Leaning on the bell, this side of hypothermia, our rescue came in the form of Sarah, Alicia's precocious daughter.

Upon entering we were subject to a sniff search by Alicia's enormous black lab. Boy is she cautious. I should have realized that with the ambulance parked at the curb and her car at the ready to give chase.

Most of the group was already there, clearly winded and tired from their uphill journey. Greeting and kiss, kiss all around. Daughter Pat sat next to our newest member Gail and I took my seat behind Cathy, my cohort on my last adventure.

After scanning the room I spied my other co-conspirator Jo sitting on the opposite couch. From what I could tell she was hoarding a bowl of cashews and slapping the hands of anyone who dared to reach for some. A knowing glance passed between us as the meeting began.

Actually it didn't as much begin as everyone just started talking at once. We were on Book Club free fall.

Gail, our neophyte, tried to take the floor, She definitely was the most vociferous and what she said wasn't necessarily relevant to the book, but she sure was interesting and enthusiastic.

Sharon and Jo-Anne were on my right with a bowl of party mix between them. They too were not into sharing and I had to have Cathy play intercept so I could grab a couple of handfuls. Geez!!

I asked Sharon how she was coping with her separation anxiety caused by her grandchildren's moving to California. She said the shock treatments and heavy drugs help somewhat but she is splitting her drugs with her husband whenever the phone bill comes in; seems she slips some into his morning oatmeal.

Val, to my left is still in her new house euphoria and was musing about window treatments. Either that or Sharon slipped some of her stash into the dip.

Debbie and Joan were busy discussing tax season and trying to convince Sharon to share her meds to ease the pain. They should have just had some dip.

Fran was quiet, probably listening to her hair grow. Now and then she'd reach for some cashews but was quickly beaten back by Jo.

Alicia was doing her hostess bit. She was pouring her favorite Chardonnay into empty and eager glasses. Fat Bastard she said, not cheap but mellow and with a smooth bouquet. She also offered a watered down Pinot Noir call Skinny Bitch.

Cathy was worried about Linda who hadn't arrived yet. She told me about Linda's penchant for Hoochie Boots even in inclement weather.

"What the heck are Hoochie Boots" She said You know the slutty spiked heeled numbers." Really? Linda? Who Knew?

Then Linda arrived, "Linda, how did you make it up the driveway, aka Mt Snow in those boots?" Everybody was dying to know.

"No Prob," she said. "I just walked backwards and dug my heels in. Used them as ice picks."

And Cathy thought they were a fashion statement. Before long we were all feeling mellow and with the spirit of camaraderie. That's when Alicia's two darling children, who were popping in and out all evening, made one last appearance before bed. While William darted behind furniture avoiding his mother's glare, Sarah was busy selling Girl Scout cookies. Some little entrepreneur got herself a record sale on venerable prey.

You know is it just a coincidence or does Alicia always has Book Club during the cookie sale??? Hmmm!!

As the evening progressed Cathy made mention of our recent escapade into the city, Jo, of course roll her eyes. Cathy's point was that we should all plan to do an adventure together. Instantly, Jo's eyes rolled straight back into her head and twitching of other body parts began. Luckily, Sharon suggesting we go by bus quelled it.

At that Jo regain her composure just in time to ward off a frontal attack on the nuts by Fran.

Onto the coffee and dessert part of the evening; we were all greatly relived when our hostess Alicia reassured us that none of the cakes and goodies were made by her. That's good or we would probably have to sign another waiver.

She did however bring out of the deep recesses of her freezer, an icy bottle of Van Gogh espresso vodka. Interesting enough on the label was Juan Valdez with his donkey. Why call it Van Gogh? That little mystery was quickly cleared up. Seems that after a couple of belts of that stuff you feel like cutting off your ear.

All to soon the evening drew to a close and everyone prepared to tackle that icy slope once more. Incredibly all were successful. Tomorrow some of us are shopping for Hoochie boots, for safety reasons of course!!

More......X's 3

Hi Kids,

Me again! Thought I'd tell you about my last Book Club meeting. Remember my previous letter when I introduced you to all my friends. Well, we had another get together last night and there were some pretty interesting goings on.

I picked up Aunt Pat and we drove the short distance to our host's house. I had a bit of a problem docking the Rocketship. I kept backing up and trying to align it properly but the dang curb kept moving. It wouldn't have been so bad except our newest member Gail had me under surveillance and was watching my maneuvers. After a few rails of laughter she proceeded to tell me how she drove her car over the curbs too. Ha Ha!!

We entered through a series of doors and were greeted by our hostess Joan. She welcomed us into her very warm and charming home. Cathy joined us shortly and commiserated over the grueling aspects of grandparenting. With one story more harrowing and exhausting after the other, we discovered that we developed a severe thirst. It was quenched by Cathy pouring us both a tall glass of white wine. More stories, more thirst and before you knew it we had a glass of wine in both hands ,our fingers wrapped tightly around the stems. I guess that's where the term two-fisted drinking originated.

Soon more of our members arrived. Debbie, Sharon, Jo-Anne Fran and Jo and we all started playing musical chairs until most of us were seated. Joan fetched a chair for the one left standing.

Before long Linda entered bring with her our long lost member, Sylvia. Seems Sylvia does square dancing instead of attending our book sessions; I was trying to figure out how she managed to be available. Rumor has it the dance hall burnt down but someone else said her does-se-doe doesn't and she was on the DL. Joan had to fetch her a chair.

Taking a good look at Linda I happened to see that she was wearing those Hoochie boots again. This time it wasn't snowing and all the ice had melted. They are a fashion statement, Hey Hey Linda!!

Finally, Val showed up looking as chic as ever. Seems she just got back from Texas where she had some poor cow skinned to give her a trendy new belt. Joan went for another chair.

Val's euphoria has lessened since our last meeting and now she regaled us with her homemaking achievements. Domestic bliss is now so routine, that even Jeff is falling asleep on the couch at 8:30PM.

My spot was between Gail and Jo. Poor Jo, she had a confrontation with her car door. She managed to shut and lock it on her thumb. Yep, she slammed the door right on that thing and flattened it. She had to unlock the car door and open it to get that sucker out. After the initial shock wore off and the pain set in, eye witnesses said that her big baby browns bulged out six inches and snapped back in and did a 360 degree roll for about five minutes, now that had to be something to see.

She was sporting a big bandage and kept her thumb sticking up all night. We couldn't figure out if she was giving the up sign or hitching a tide. Pity touched us all and we even handed her the nuts.

Fran was appointed moderator for the evening and definitely had her work cut out for her, Trying to get and keep the attention of 13 yapping women was no small task but she handled herself well and we started discussing the month's book selection.

Joan was darting back and forth between the kitchen and us.. She was done fetching chairs and topping off everyone's wine glass. She made mention that she hadn't made any of the evening's refreshments. Nope, Joan singlehandedly tried to jumpstart the economy by buying everything and not only that she did it with a 50% off coupon. Way to go Joan, you are a great American!

The conversation was moving right along when somehow we got into the subject of scent recognition. I told you it's hard tto stay on track. We were in Book Club free fall and Fran just rolled her eyes. Oh no!! It must be catching!

Daughter Pat said whenever she smells the sweet scent of pot it reminds her of her college days and dorm. Did she forget I was 6 feet away? Next Jo said whenever she smells bleach she gets a flashback of leaving her kids with a convicted felon. Seems she hired him to babysit and the man's favorite cologne was Eau di Clorox. You know Jo, you are starting to worry me.

Val piped in saying that she was such a goody two shoes that she never even tried pot until she was forty. Somehow I get the picture of her trying to make up for lost time. There she is sitting on the couch, smoking like a fiend, no wonder Jeff is nodding off. All that second hand smoke; maybe not, my imagination is on overdrive.

As stories about pot were circulation around the room I couldn't help but notice all the sideward glances and sly smiles. The biggest revelation of all came from Sharon. She became quite animated and told us about an incident from her youth. Seems she was pitting her hair up in curlers when an irresistible urge for a cigarette took hold of her. Realizing she didn't have any she went to her brother's room to borrow one. He wasn't there but his cigarette case was. She opened it and was surprised they didn't have any filters. I guess the fact that they were twisted eluded her. She took one and returned to her room to light up, having a hair clip with a feather to help her hold it was just a coincidence. She professes ignorance and said she no memory of getting high. However she did remark that if marijuana ever became legal she was going to buy it by the carton.

I wonder what the brand names would be? Lucky Highs… Really Kool… Bet-cha Sweet Grass??? Sorry, my imagination is out of control.

Thank goodness Alicia didn't come. Being an officer f the court she would probably have to report us, have us patted down and then defend us! She certainly knows how to get business.

Speaking of business, we were sidelined again buy Gail's questioning us about our occupations. She's new and with all that talk of pot she may have thought one of us was a dealer. Sorry Gail, just educators, CPA's, lawyer, health care professional and businesswomen. However maybe we can get Sharon to introduce you to her brother.

Meanwhile, Joan is fetching Sylvia more refills and trying to get the meeting back from the brink of chaos. She interrupts the clamor by getting us to pick next month's book and announces that coffee is served. Good save Joan. (She probably can't wait for us to leave.)Enjoying our desserts and coffee as the evening ore down, I had one more conversation with Jo.

I seems that she and her husband Paul, together with some friends went out to dinner. She had a 50% coupon for Ladies night on Tuesday at a local eaterie. If you sit at the bar you and your guests are entitled to the discount. As Jo tells it the bar was crowded and the overspill was seated in the dining room, she and her guests dined there.

Thinking the same offer applied she was shocked to discover that she was the only on discounted. It was sort of a bait and switch.

I told her that she should fix their wagon. Next Tuesday she should have Paul and all his friends dress up in drag and get the discount. That should fix their wagon!!

Well, we called it a night and left , Joan was busy fetching back all the chairs. Cathy was encouraging me to learn how to do attachments on the computer. I can drive the Rocketship, take care of Lucey write goofy letters .. there's just so much one person can do.

I'm thinking I'll send this letter when you graduate college. your Moms will cut off my grandmother visits if I don't. TMI!!!

MORE ....X's 4

Hi Guys,

Well another month, another Book Club meeting. This time Aunt Pat was behind the wheel. She had it easy, no blinding snowstorms, no ice hills to conquer, no pesky moving curbs. We made our journey in record time and she successfully docked her Rocketship. Actually that thing is as big as a space station.

We started down the path to our hostess Fran's apartment when suddenly we heard a car pull up, door opened and slammed then it sped off. Turning we saw Cathy coming down the path towards us. "Were you in that car Cathy?" "Oh, yeah, Mario just dropped me off." I asked, "What's his hurry?" "Oh, he's running late, he's going to Calandra's with Paul for Ladies Night." "Remember Pat, it was your idea. Every Tuesday they dress in drag and get the 50% off Ladies special."

"Oh yeah, so why are they late?" I wanted to know. Cathy then told us that Mario had trouble with his tights and Paul's wig wouldn't stay on. Mario solved it by shaving his hairy legs and going barelegged and the he Gorilla glued the wig to Paul's head. "Well, that should do it and we moved on."

As we approached Fran's front door we face our first dilemma. There were two doorbells one atop the other. Fran lives in a garden apartment, she's on the first floor with a neighbor above her. Which doorbell to ring? I being the most logical one of our group said the bottom one; bottom floor, bottom bell, logical. " Not so fast." Aunt Pat cautioned. "What if we ring the wrong bell and disturb her neighbor!?"

"It might be a sweet little old lady who's taking a nap?" "Don't be ridiculous," I replied, "Sweet little old ladies are asleep at 8PM, ring the bell!" Cathy stopped me, "Hold on, what if it is an axe murderer, sharpening his blade and watching reruns of Saturday Night Massacre?"

"We wouldn't want to tick him off would we?"

"Actually that's a good point there, Cathy, good thinking. "

As we stood there, Aunt Pat came up with an idea. She said, "Let's do Ding, Dong, Ditch." That's where you ring a door bell, run off and hide and watch to see who opens the door." I know the game well, Little Christopher does it to all my neighbors when he stays by me. They are taking a petition to keep him out of the complex. "Let's not, besides I can't run too fast," I volunteered.

Next, Cathy suggested a coin toss. Another discussion broke out to decide what would be heads and what would be tails. As logical as ever I maintained that heads for the top floor and tails for the bottom. Logical! But Pat and Cathy said that was too discriminatory. Another plan shelved.

I looked over at Cathy and saw that her eyes had glazed over and then she began to speak in an unworldly voice. "What if you rang a doorbell and no one is home? Would it make a noise?" "Snap out of it Cathy, don't go all existential on us .We are in crisis mode here. Happy Hour is passing us by!"

From our viewpoint on the steps we could see the revelers inside, oblivious to our misery outside. While we in our darkest despair the door suddenly opened. There was Jo asking us what we were doing out there? When we told her of our indecision she said that the front door was open and we could have walked right in a knocked on Fran's door. "Don't want to disturb the axe murderer upstairs you know." whew!! That was close!

After some hasty Hello-s we three rushed to the bar to make up for lost time. Fortified with my Chardonnay, I paid a proper greeting to our hostess, Fran "I swear, Fran that your hair has grown 6 inches since last month. How do you do it? I have to know. The hair on my legs grows faster than on my head. Is it vitamins, minerals, or Rogaine? Please tell me," I was begging. Fran just smile sweetly and moved on. Drats!!

Next I saw Jo. "Hi Jo, stick in your fingers in any car doors lately?"

"No!" she said. Then she whipped out the blackest thumb I ever saw. "Oh, my gosh, Jo keep that thing away from plants, It's a lethal weapon, you'll set the Green Movement back 30 years." She gave me a quizzical look and she too moved on.

I went to my seat, passing Linda. "Hey, hey Linda, what's shaking? Hold on a minute, are you Okay? Where are the Hoochie Boots?" "Oh them? They're at the cobbler's, he's putting toe peeps in. Now that it's spring I want to make them more fashionable." "Oh, Linda my hero, how could I ever doubt you?" I replied.

I took my spot next to Gail. She was sitting in her chair with the straightest back I ever saw. Wow, what posture! I noticed that she was clutching her handbag as if she was in the subway at rush hour. "Don't worry, Gail," I tried to assure her. "We are all peace loving here, your bag is safe." Almost reluctantly she put it down next to her.

My curious mind thought it was strange. Me thinks she might be recording us. After last meeting she was asking a lot of questions. Names, job titles where to get pot. I'll have to keep my eye on her.

Glancing to my left I saw Linda writing out a check and handing it to Jo. Aha!! So Jo is already extorting money to stay away from peoples' gardens; all that in plain view of Alicia. That Jo is something else.

Our discussion started again, Fran narrated. She sat serenely and asked questions. All around us we ranted and raved. No one liked the book. We were becoming hostile. Fran just sat there calmly; all that hair growth and nerves of steel too. I needed to know her secret a plan was forming in my mind.

Meanwhile, everyone wanted to know the culprit that suggested our despised read. Then we remembered, it was square dancing, Sylvia.

Seems her does-si-doe was better and she was swinging swing left and right again.

With the commotion in full force I made my move. I proceeded to Fran's powder room. I intended to take a look inside her medicine cabinet. I had to know her secret. I was stricken with a pang of conscience. Should I or shouldn't I? It was be an act of invasion of privacy, it would be rude, it would be… Oh but the hair, the serenity, the temptation was too great.

I reached up and tried the door. It wouldn't open. I tried again. No luck. Then I saw it. Uh oh!! A keypad lock and oops… a blinking red light. Oh no!! The thing was alarmed. I quickly shut off the bathroom light and high tailed it out of there as fast as I could. I don't think anyone missed me. I was praying the alarm didn't go off. What stress!!

Luck was with me, no alarm sounded. My reputation was still intact. I'll never do that again. However…why does she have it alarmed and locked? See, there is a secret.

Discussion over, it was time for sweet treats. My pounding

heart was just beginning to slow and I took comfort in knowing it wasn't my imagination with the hair thing. I'll wear you down some how Fran. Maybe I'll wave Jo's black thumb at her. Maybe I'll whisper something into Gail's pocketbook alluding to Fran's mysterious potion. Maybe I'll bribe Fran out of sight of Alicia. I have to think on this.

Book Club adjoined and I headed home with Aunt Pat. I asked her to come with me next Tuesday on Ladies Night to check out Mario and Paul. Later...Yia

MORE....X's 5

Greeting Fellow Travelers,

A report on the latest Rocketship adventures. I want to state right off that it was a complete success. But of course!!!

It started the night before where the crew and I met with the rest of our support group. It was under the disguise of a Book Club dinner but I know if was actually a send of celebration. While we feasted and raised our glasses in friendship; I looked over and made a startling discovery.

Seated to my left was Fran....you know the one with the hair I mention her all the time. I decided tonight not to comment on it. Thought I might be becoming annoying. Well, would you believe that after a while a very disappointed Fran turns to me and says, "Don't you like my new haircut? You always say such nice things about my hair."

"What Frannie, you got it cut?" I was astounded. It looked longer than the last time I saw her, which was 4 weeks ago. "Oh yes," she replied, "took off about 6 inches." "SIX INCHES?????Your hair grows that fast?" I was stuttering. "my nails too," was her answer.

At that rate she must be related to Edward Scissorhands or... could it be, a sleeper cell from another galaxy? It's hard to imagine a human with such growth ability. Then looking down the table I realized that Sharon too, had similar hair capability, this puts a whole new light on things. Okay, someone or something is watching our movements.

Obviously these two fine women are not yet aware of this. I will be on guard and keep then under my surveillance.

I met with my cockpit crew at the end of our celebration and confirmed the time and place for departure. Mission is ready to go!!

Next day began bright and sunny, perfect weather for a flight. I picked up Cathy, my co-pilot at her home base. We went over the instruments and flight plan. She suggested we reverse thrusters to get Jo on board. I pointed out that a straight trajectory was more efficient, Cathy, my Co immediately concurred and the chain of command was promptly reestablished.

Linda our newest crew member got on next, then I did a 180 and Jo completed our team. Jo's husband Paul suggested that we should be careful and observant of those sneaky signs they erect. Good thinking Paul! We immediately gave Linda that assignment. Paul must have worked for Mission Control at sometime. Who knows, maybe he still does.

We were off. Traveling at warp speed down Bloomfield Avenue we arrived at our destination. Now on to docking. I navigated the ship into a tight area. I had trouble with straight alignment because if the LEM next to me. My Co-Cathy said it was a smart car. It actually looked like a Fred Flintstone throw back. However you can't fool the Rocketship. It was trying to attach it.

Twice I maneuvered the ship around. No use! I exited the craft and spied a cute humanoid approaching. He greeted us and I immediately detected a foreign tongue. "Where do you come from," I queried? Eitailly came the answer. Eitailly, Eitailly isn't that a planet in the southern hemisphere? Hmm.

I reentered the vehicle as my new Eitaillian friend took over the stern and Linda the aft and directed my maneuvers. No use. Autopilot kept coming on and the Rocketship kept trying to attach the LEM.

I changed my course of action and redirected the ship to another mooring. Once docked, I disembarked and joined the crew. The Eitraillian was congratulating my group on their bravery. I'm so proud of them.

Needing substance, we had a leisurely lunch and discussed our past adventures and made plans for future forays into the unknown. Next, on to our objective.

Leaving the mess hall, we trudged on foot up a steep incline tat would put Mt. Everest to shame. Cathy and Jo took the lead with Linda and me bring up the flank. We reached the summit and although we had no flag to plant, we all praised ourselves on this accomplishment. After sucking in a fresh supply of oxygen and lowering our heart rates, we entered the hallow halls of the Montclair Museum. Our interest was the three generations of Wyeth artists.

We strolled slowly through the serene rooms featuring a mix of still lives, portraits, landscapes and modern art; all so very impressive.

Finally we saw the main feature. N.C., Andrew and Jamie Wyeth. Genes really do count. Most the art there was owned by the Bank of America; so that's where all the bailout money went.

Fully culturally sated, we joined forces in the rotunda and planned our exit strategy. We decided to leave via the lower level exit. Before reaching the door we encountered that Etaillian again. Said he work for the museum. Yeah, sure right! A cell if ever I saw one. I wonder if his hair has that rapid growth syndrome?

We boarded the ship for our return voyage home. Buckled up, we blasted off. I was pleased that Linda did great on her maiden voyage. Cathy said she was in need of some liquid refreshment and a nap and Jo gave up her rosary beads, Good to see Jo gaining such confidence.

I brought my crew back to their Farrington home base, Gave a knowing nod to Paul, who was waiting for Jo's arrival and I bade farewell to Linda and Cathy.

Like I said a very successful mission. I directed the ship onward to my command Center where I planned to do research on Eitailly and Eitaillians. Maybe a destination for our next mission.

To infinity and wherever.….

Acknowledgements
With Gratitude

I am so very Blessed to have in my life a supportive family and friends.

My stepson Michael who did all the interior illustrations and my grandson John who did the book cover. Both immensely talented who contributed their gifts to give life to the zany characters.

Shirley reappears as Yia's best friend and cohort in adventures. This based on my dear friend Marsha Diamond who fills that bill in real life.

We have a standing Friday night date where we wonder how we lost our misspent youth.

The staff at Outskirts Press whose authors representative Colleen Goulet has guided this work to fruition. Thank you all again.

CPSIA information can be obtained
at www.ICGtesting.com
Printed in the USA
BVHW031424220819
556562BV00003B/11/P